Tucker and Co
Stories of Life In and Out of Grange Hill

What's Tucker Jenkins up to skulking around
Grange Hill? Is it possible that he's losing his usual
confidence? Surely not. Yet his rebellious attack on
Mr Sutcliffe doesn't have its desired effect, and
lands Tucker in deeper trouble than he bargained
for. And on top of this, life outside Grange Hill is
becoming difficult too. Even Tucker's friends, Alan,
Tommy and Benny can't understand what's got into
him. Meanwhile, first formers Zammo and Jonah
are learning the hard way how to survive at Grange
Hill: keep out of Gripper Stebson's path – but if you
can't, retaliate. And although Annette Firman
thinks she's too tough to be got at, she doesn't
realize that her classmates have finally decided
something must be done to put her in her place.

Other books about Grange Hill
by Robert Leeson in Fontana Lions

GRANGE HILL RULES O.K.?
GRANGE HILL GOES WILD
GRANGE HILL FOR SALE

PHIL REDMOND

Tucker and Co

*Stories of Life
In and Out of Grange Hill*

Based on the BBC television series
GRANGE HILL

FONTANA·LIONS

First published in Fontana Lions 1982 by
William Collins Sons & Co. Ltd
14 St James's Place, London SW1
Second Impression June 1982

© Philip Redmond 1982

Printed in Great Britain by
William Collins Sons & Co. Ltd, Glasgow

Contents

Vengeance

Jonah sank his teeth into his Mars bar, tore off the end and mashed the chunk of 'work, rest and play' into a semi-liquid mass, smooth enough to slide down his throat. By the time he was ready for a second attack, Zammo had polished his off.

'Why don't you eat the paper and all?' Jonah asked, with just a hint of disgust in his voice. The one thing he'd never got used to in all the years he'd known Zammo was his eating habits.

'Don't like the taste,' Zammo replied, almost sounding serious.

'It wouldn't be in your mouth long enough for you to notice.'

'At least I don't look like a bleedin' cow when I'm eating,' Zammo countered. 'It's supposed to be a snack, you know. Why do you always make a meal out of everything you eat?'

Jonah pulled a face at Zammo's lousy joke, took another bite and let his eyes wander about the playground. They'd only been at Grange Hill for a couple of days, but already they had learned the two golden rules for survival. Sit with your back to a wall and keep your eyes on the move. They'd already had one brush with Gripper Stebson, now the unchallenged school headcase, and Jonah didn't fancy the idea of another. He turned to Zammo. 'How'd you reckon this Gripper fellah got his nickname?'

'Grips you where you wouldn't show your mother.' Zammo shrugged. 'So they reckon. Like to see him try it on me.' Zammo was his usual pugnacious self. They had known each other since the infants and Jonah had never known Zammo to walk away from a fight. Even if he was outnumbered or it was with older boys. Trouble was, it meant Jonah had to get involved too, so over the years he had mastered two other basic survival skills: a good turn of speed, and the gift of the gab. If Jonah couldn't either run or talk his way out of a problem, it really was a problem.

'What we going to do now?' Zammo asked, now bored.

'I haven't finished me Mars yet.'

'If we wait for that, we'll be here till half-three. Let's go and explore a bit.'

'Do we have to?'

'Yeah . . . c'mon.' Zammo was actually on his feet when the shadow fell on them. Jonah looked up but couldn't make out who it was because the sun was immediately behind him. However, the worn and scuffed DM's gave him a clue and a quick look at Zammo's worried face confirmed the fact, even before one of the DM's whipped out and kicked him on the thigh.

'Ain't you got no respect?' The voice was all too familiar. 'Get up when King Gripper's talking to you.' It was Stebson. Jonah peeled himself off the wall and stood up. He was only halfway up when the remains of his Mars bar were prised out of his hand. Stebson broke off the end Jonah had been eating, tossed it in the

10

air and volleyed it towards a third-year football match as it fell.

'Don't want to catch any of your germs,' he grinned, as he stuffed the remainder into his mouth. If Jonah's eating habits irritated Zammo, Gripper's made him feel ill. He chewed the food around his open mouth, speaking as he did so.

'You first years?'

'Er . . . yes,' Jonah replied.

'What's it got to do with you?' Zammo asked, then wished he hadn't, as Gripper's hand was suddenly gripped around Zammo's left ear. The pain was almost unbearable; Zammo now appreciated the aptness of the nickname. It was almost impossible to believe that anyone could squeeze so hard with just one hand, but the agony down the left side of his head convinced him . . .

'Aaarrgghh . . . get off!'

'I never heard you say you were sorry.'

'What for . . . aarrgghh!' Gripper tightened the hold.

'All right . . . I'm sorry.'

'Sorry, what?'

'Er . . . very sorry . . . Owww . . .'

'Use my full title.'

'Sorry . . . er King Gripper.' Zammo squealed. He was having difficulty in holding back the tears.

'Sorry, your Highness, King Gripper.'

'Sorry . . . your . . . Highness, King Gripper.'

'And you won't be disrespectful again?'

'No . . . honest . . . aarrgghh.' Zammo squealed again as Gripper gave one last twist that forced a tear out of Zammo's eye.

'Not crying are you?' Gripper bent close to have a look.

11

'No!' Zammo replied quickly, instinctively brushing his eyes with his sleeve. Gripper grabbed his arm.

'You're not used to it, see.' He then took hold of Jonah's ear. 'Like your mate here.' He squeezed until Jonah too squealed. 'I run courses for kids like you. Toughen you up, like. So you don't become cry-babies. Interested?'

'Yes, your Highness, King Gripper.' Jonah was never slow to catch on. Gripper grinned and relaxed his grip. He could see Jonah obviously had respect.

'Want to sign on then?'

'Er . . . yes,' Jonah replied.

'Thought you might. They're very popular this year. Specially among you first years. There's a queue to join.'

'I'm not surprised,' moaned Zammo, still rubbing his ear.

'Yeah . . . but they're also expensive to run. Overheads and that. So I have to ask for a small donation. Get my meaning?' They both did, but neither was in a hurry to push in front of the other for this particular queue.

Jonah took a quick look round, but there was no way out. The back to the wall rule had prevented that, curbing the use of his running skill, while Gripper wasn't exactly the sort you could talk out of breaking your legs if he had set his mind on it. There was only one way out.

'How much?' he heard himself ask.

Gripper grinned. 'Half of what you've got. I ain't greedy.' But then his grin widened. 'So long as it doesn't come to less than twenty pence.'

Jonah dug into his pocket. He only had fifteen pence left after buying the Mars bar.

'That'll do, seeing as it's your first time.'

Gripper turned to Zammo. 'What you got?'

Zammo hesitated for a moment. It was asking too much of him simply to give in like this. Jonah could see Zammo was about to resist and quickly nudged him. Zammo took the hint. This was no time for heroics. He handed over twenty out of the twenty-five pence he had in his pocket.

'And the other five,' Gripper said, then grinned again. 'To make up what your mate owes me.'

Reluctantly Zammo handed it over. Gripper took their money and turned to walk away, but stopped.

'Well? What do you say when I'm going?'

'Er . . . Goodbye, your Highness, King Gripper,' Jonah said quickly, hoping he had guessed right. He had. Gripper grinned. 'You won't need many lessons,' he said to Jonah, but then punched Zammo in the stomach causing him to double over in pain and fall to the floor. 'But you might need a bit of extra tuition.' With that, he finally swaggered off in search of other prey.

Jonah let out a long sigh as he bent to help Zammo get up.

'That was the worst few minutes of my life, that was.'

'How'd you think I felt?' Zammo gasped.

'You all right?'

'No thanks to you. Yes your Highness. No your Highness.'

'What else was I supposed to do? And we would have ended in a worse state if I hadn't, pimple brain.'

Zammo nodded. He knew Jonah was right and that he was angry that he'd cried in front of Gripper. 'I'll tell you something though, Jonah,' Zammo suddenly said, 'he's not going to get any twenty pence a week out of me!'

'What are you going to do about it?'

'Dunno . . . but he's not going to get away with it.' Zammo picked up his bag and turned for the Science Block as the bell sounded for the end of break. Jonah picked up his own bag and followed. He was worried. Not about the fact that Zammo was planning to defy Gripper, but by the fact that he was out for revenge. It wasn't just that he was convinced it could only end in a beating. But although Zammo was the one who wanted to make a stand, it would be Jonah he would expect to think of the way to do it. What was even worse was the fact that Jonah knew he'd have to be the one to do it.

With only Miss Mooney's science lesson to cope with after the break, Zammo's mind wasn't sufficiently taxed to prevent him thinking about Gripper.

'Why do you reckon nutjobs like Gripper carry on like they do?' Zammo whispered to Jonah.

'Because they've got something missing,' Jonah replied but he wasn't really interested. The less he knew about Gripper the better.

'It's not right though, is it?' Zammo continued. 'We all have to watch it in case he jumps us. Someone should put the bubble in.'

'Like you, you mean?'

But Zammo didn't get a chance to reply. 'Gordon Jones and Samuel McGuire! What did I just say?'

Miss Mooney's squeaky voice came floating across the room from behind her tangled mass of scientific equipment.

'Er . . what did I just say, miss?' Jonah stalled, hoping someone would whisper the answer.

'Don't act the fool with me, Jones.'

14

'He doesn't have to act, miss,' Annette Firman was quick to add. Jonah glared across at her. He'd never liked her since he first saw her.

'Well, Jones?' Jonah looked blank. He hadn't a clue what she'd been talking about.

'What about you, McGuire? Perhaps you could make a more inspired guess?'

'Er . . . you mean just now, miss?' Zammo too hoped someone would whisper something, but nobody did. They hadn't known anyone long enough yet.

'No! Last Tuesday,' Miss Mooney said, sarcastically. 'As neither of you seem to be paying attention, I suggest you both stand out in the corridor for the rest of the lesson and allow other people more willing to learn to get on with it.'

Jonah and Zammo exchanged a look, then sloped off towards the door.

'And before you leave, you will come and see me so we can organize some additional homework for you. So you can catch up. Now, outside please.'

The last thing Jonah saw as he closed the door was Annette, a huge grin across her face. She always seemed to enjoy other people's misery. A right trouble-maker she is, Jonah thought as he stuck out his tongue and closed the door.

'Now look what you've got me into,' he moaned to Zammo as they both flopped against the wall.

'It weren't my fault! You was talking just as much as me.'

'You started it. Going on about that Gripper bloke.'

Zammo had no answer to that, so Jonah walked across to a window.

'It's stupid this, isn't it?' Zammo suddenly asked.

15

'What is?'

'This. Sending us out of a lesson as a punishment. I mean, half the time we'd do anything to get out of lessons, and all you've got to do is talk and they do it for you.' He shrugged. 'Stupid if you ask me.'

'It's not this, is it?' Jonah replied. 'It's having to do the extra work at home that's the real pain.'

'Yeah,' Zammo nodded. Jonah was right. The one thing he detested above everything about school was doing homework. As far as Zammo was concerned, once the bell went at the end of the afternoon, that should be the end of school for the day. Unless, of course, he wanted to play football or go to the swimming club or something like that. Like the sports trials later in the week. But that was different.

They stood in silence for a moment before another horrible thought popped into Zammo's head.

'Think she'll give us detention as well?'

'Doubt it. Think she'd have done that in there. At least, I hope she would.' He didn't sound too sure. However, what was done was done and Zammo turned his mind towards other things.

'You going to these sports trial things?'

'Shouldn't think so,' Jonah replied. He wasn't all that keen on sport.

'C'mon, it'll be good.'

'How do you know?'

'It just will,' Zammo said enthusiastically, as he always did if he wanted to do anything. 'C'mon, I know you're rubbish, but you can watch me.'

'Doing what?'

'Running. I'm good at that.'

'Pity you don't do it more often, then. So we wouldn't end up in aggro with the likes of Gripper

16

Stebson, or be standing out here now. Anyway, you might not be able to go.'

'Why not?'

'Because you might be in detention, mightn't you?'

'You said she wouldn't . . .' Zammo started to speak, but he did not finish his sentence. Suddenly a voice boomed out along the corridor, making the prospect of detention more real.

'And what are you boys doing, standing here?'

The voice belonged to Mr Curtis, the Head of the First Year and one of the cane-everything-that-moves-or-answers-back brigade. Jonah had heard someone say that Curtis was in a Territorial Army Parachute Regiment at the weekends. As he marched up the corridor towards them, Jonah could believe it. He certainly looked like an apprentice Action Man.

'Er . . . nothing, sir,' Zammo managed to reply.

'Nothing? Shouldn't you be doing *something*, lad, like the odd lesson or two, perhaps?'

Zammo turned to Jonah with one of his 'Talk us out of this' looks. Thanks a lot, thought Jonah, as he cleared his throat. It had suddenly gone dry at the sight of Curtis and his tongue felt like a huge roll of sandpaper.

'Er . . . we're waiting for Miss Mooney, sir,' Jonah offered. It wasn't exactly a lie, more a slight distortion of the truth.

'Waiting for her?' Curtis bent forward, his nose about half-an-inch from Jonah's.

God, his breath stinks, thought Jonah as he tried to back away; but he found his head banging against the wall behind him. For the second time that day he had been caught against a wall. So much for the Grange Hill golden rules. 'Er . . . yes, sir.'

17

'Why?' Curtis asked. It seemed like a reasonable question.

'Er . . . she told us to, sir.' Which didn't seem like a reasonable reply, as Curtis's knuckle rapped smartly on Jonah's head.

'Why?' Curtis asked again. Jonah took a sideways glance across at Zammo. He looked as though he was about to wet himself. Arguing with other kids, whether older or outnumbered, was a completely different situation from having to face someone like Curtis. Jonah's attention was soon pulled back to Curtis by a sharp knuckle on his head and another wave of foul breath. 'Eyes front when I'm talking to you, lad. Why did Miss Mooney tell you to wait here?' Curtis's knuckle emphasized each word as though he was trying to drive the message through the top of Jonah's skull.

'Er . . . she wants to talk about some additional er . . .' Jonah had to be careful choosing the right word. He knew if he said homework it would sound suspicious, yet he had to be careful not to lie in case they were found out, which would only make matters worse. His first thought was to use the word work, but dismissed it as still sounding too much like a punishment.

He could see Curtis's eyes change and felt him drawing breath. Any moment another wave of stench would envelop him as he asked why Jonah was hesitating. The word tuition arrived on Jonah's tongue. It was exactly what he was looking for.'. . . er . . . she wants to talk to us about some additional tuition, sir.' It sounded good, Jonah thought. As though they were simply in need of extra attention rather than punishment. Jonah could see the eyes register the phrase, and half accept the explanation. But Curtis was too old a hand to let it go at that. The stench returned.

'Additional tuition?'

'Yes, sir. We er . . . didn't do science at our last school.' (That was true.) 'And we're er . . . a bit behind the rest of our class.' (That too was true, even if it was only ten minutes behind.) 'So she er . . . asked us to see her at the end of this lesson.' (That also was true.)

There was still a flicker of doubt in Curtis's eyes, but Jonah had been at his most convincing and just at that moment the bell sounded for changeover. It seemed as though they had finished early somewhere else and had come along, as ordered, to see Miss Mooney.

Curtis straightened up. Jonah let out a low sigh and breathed through his nose again. It looked as if Curtis had swallowed it. Especially as his attention was caught by the rest of N1 coming out of the Science Lab in a disorganized mass to join the incoming tide of bodies flowing along the corridor.

Curtis could never resist the temptation to form a disorderly mass into organized, disciplined lines. It was probably the Action Man in him.

'Single file. On the left. Walk, don't run!' he bellowed down the corridor, and as if by magic the sea of bodies parted and people found themselves pulled to the sides of the corridor and two organized, disciplined lines flowed past each other. Curtis smiled. That was the way he liked things.

Jonah and Zammo exchanged a look of relief as Curtis turned and started to walk away. Their faces were just breaking into grins when Miss Mooney came out. 'Right. Now let's decide on a suitable punishment for you two.'

Jonah's heart sank. His spine went rigid as though someone had just dropped a dozen ice cubes down the back of his shirt. Without even turning he could sense

Curtis had stopped. Even at twenty metres, Curtis's highly-tuned antennae would pick up a word like *punishment*. Jonah's own antennae were working well, as Curtis returned.

'Did you say punishment, Miss Mooney?'

'Yes,' she wasn't sure why it concerned him, but she continued, 'for talking during my lesson.'

'I see,' said Curtis as his executioner's grin came to his face.

'So they were sent outside, were they?'

'Yes.'

Jonah and Zammo exchanged another look, only this time of horror, as Curtis bent forward and this time his nose touched Jonah's. 'Well, well, well, m'laddo. I'd say you were in trouble, wouldn't you?'

And I'd say you need to see a dentist, was all Jonah could think of.

They had missed the cane by millimetres and only due to the intervention of Miss Mooney. She knew that because of her forgetful, nervous manner she had become something of a joke with the rest of the staff. She knew that she *was* occasionally too soft, but she thought that preferable to the bully-boy tactics adopted by the likes of Curtis. It was this reason alone that saved Jonah and Zammo from the cane. Miss Mooney refused to allow Curtis to interfere with the way she ran her lessons. In spite of the fact that Curtis claimed they had deliberately lied to him, Miss Mooney insisted that they were her responsibility. Reluctantly he had given in, not wanting to get into an argument in front of the boys and pleased that Miss Mooney had learned at long last that all they ever need is a good thumping every now and then.

Fortunately for Jonah and Zammo, Miss Mooney had not decided to adopt the Curtis method, but resorted to her own particular preference of denying them their free time. So the next evening Jonah and Zammo were booked in for their first spell of detention.

It wasn't so much the detention that was the problem, nor even having to tell their mums why they would be late, but the fact that Gripper Stebson was, as always, there as well. He was all right, well, tolerable, during detention, but as soon as they left, Jonah and Zammo found Gripper's hand squeezing their ears and their own hands digging into their pockets and handing over 20p each.

'That does it,' Zammo said as he tried to rub the pain away. 'We got sent to detention because of him.'

'Because you were talking in class, you mean.'

'I was talking about *him*, wasn't I?' Zammo corrected. 'And then when we get here, he's here – and does us again. He's not going to get away with it, you know.'

Jonah couldn't prevent a slight smile at Zammo's predictability. 'He just did, didn't he?' he replied as he started for home, also rubbing his ear vigorously.

'Well, he won't do it again, then.'

'How you going to stop him?'

'We'll think of something, won't we?'

The use of 'we' was not lost on Jonah.

'He might leave us alone now,' Jonah suggested, not believing it for one moment.

Zammo's expression told him he didn't believe it either.

'We can't let him get away with it, Jonah, or he'll just keep stinging us otherwise. I mean, if we have to stump

21

up 20p every time we see him, we're going to be constantly skint! Even if we have the bread in the first place. We've got to fight back.'

'Yeah,' Jonah agreed, 'but how?'

It wasn't until later in the week, at the sports trials, that a possible answer to that question came up.

While Jonah and Zammo were wandering about, waiting for the track running events for which Zammo had entered, they spotted Gripper offering some slimming advice to the fat boy in their form, Roland Browning. The essence of Gripper's advice was not to eat sweets and, not surprisingly, to give them to him instead. Although they didn't know Roland too well, they felt sorry for him because he was such a natural and easy victim for Gripper. However, they kept out of the way, not wanting any more trouble themselves.

Although Zammo turned in a good performance, he was not outstanding, and would have to wait until later to see if he would be selected for the school team. Jonah was now more than ready to get home.

However, just as they turned towards the showers, their hearts missed a beat. Gripper was lurking in the gym doorway, leaning against the wall, chewing a match, and from the grin on his face he was obviously waiting for them.

'What now?' Jonah moaned as they slowed down.

'Know what day it is?' Gripper asked.

'No, what?'

'Pay day.'

'We gave you 20p the other night,' Zammo protested.

Gripper straightened himself, ready to make a grab

for them. 'That was for extras. This is your regular payment.'

'We're skint.'

'Then you'll have to find some from somewhere, won't you? Or don't you want any more lessons in survival?'

As he spoke his arm shot forward, but both Jonah and Zammo had had enough survival lessons to see it coming. In one movement they both jumped back.

'Run!' shouted Jonah, but Zammo was three paces away already as Gripper made a lunge for Jonah who, without even realizing it, swung his foot out and kicked Gripper. 'You little . . . !' Gripper exclaimed.

Of course, Gripper was after them like a rocket. For an instant he was stunned that anyone, let alone first years, would defy him never mind actually kick him. But he soon recovered enough to want to teach them a lesson. No one disobeys King Gripper.

'Come here, you!' he roared as he rounded the corner.

'Flippin' 'eck, Jonah! What'd you do that for?' Zammo moaned as they dashed across the playground towards the bike sheds.

'Come here!' Gripper was still screaming as they reached the bike sheds, sped through, swinging on the iron railings that led up the steps to the main teaching block, and crashed against the swing doors into the main corridor.

Gripper was closing the gap. He smashed through just in time to see Zammo turn up the stairs. He stopped. At the top of the staircase there was only the library and a few classrooms, and Gripper knew they wouldn't go into any of the rooms as they would be trapped.

They would keep going along the corridor, but because of his superior knowledge of the school's geography, they were trapped anyway. He didn't go up the staircase, but continued towards the far end of the block.

Gripper was right. As Jonah came bounding up the stairs, one look was sufficient to tell him that every room was a trap. They had to keep going. 'Come on,' he called. 'Straight on.' The way Jonah was keeping up the pace he should have entered for the running trials and not Zammo, who was now beginning to fall behind. By this time they were along the corridor and about to grab the banister rail and swing down the stairs, when Jonah looked back to make sure Zammo was still with him. He froze. He stopped so suddenly that Zammo crashed into his back.

'Hang about,' Jonah said. 'Look.'

Zammo turned. There was no sign of Gripper, who a moment before had been snapping at their heels.

'Where is he?' Zammo asked.

'Ssshhhh!' It was quiet. Too quiet. Jonah moved to the stairwell and leaned over to see if he could see or hear anything from below. Nothing. Zammo looked worried. He began to speak but Jonah put his fingers to his lips. They both stood listening. Their panting for breath appeared to echo and resonate throughout the empty building. Empty, that is, apart from them – and Gripper.

Where was he?

A similar thought was going through Gripper's mind. He had positioned himself beneath the stairs, nicely placed so that he could jump them as they came down. His grin had grown wider as he heard their pounding feet come closer and closer until they suddenly stopped. Now his grin had faded. He, too, was twisting his head trying to pick up any sound. They were, in fact, standing about two metres above his head.

Neither Jonah nor Zammo appeared to be breathing as they hovered on the landing. Jonah leaned close to Zammo's ear.

'He must be down there.'

Zammo nodded. He then tapped Jonah and jerked his head back the way they came. If Gripper had headed them off, all they had to do was double back. Carefully, trying not to make a sound, they slowly back-tracked along the corridor.

They didn't make a sound, which was what alerted Gripper. The cogs began to turn in his head. If they hadn't come crashing down the stairs as they should have done, they'd obviously stopped. They'd have realized he wasn't behind them, and soon figured out that he'd gone to cut them off. Then they'd have realized he'd be waiting where he was and . . . He quietly crept out of the stairwell and headed back towards the other stairs.

Jonah and Zammo were now halfway down. Jonah looked at Zammo for reassurance. All Zammo could do was shrug. He didn't know if Gripper was down there or not. So Jonah took a deep breath and started down. Just as he was going, Zammo grabbed his shoulder and pointed frantically at the corner of the wall.

Jonah's heart stopped. There, just sticking out, was the scuffed toe-cap of a pair of DM's. They turned and charged back up the stairs. At the sound of the scramble, the toe-cap jerked into life and came round the corner showing it was indeed a Gripper foot. This time he didn't try any subtle manoeuvres, but went straight up the stairs after them.

The chase went on. Up the stairs. Along the corridor. Down the stairs. Back along the main corridor. Through the doors. Through the bike sheds. Across the playground. Back towards the gym – with no sign of Gripper either catching them, or letting them go – until they came into sight of Bullet Baxter. 'You boys!' he roared from the gym door. 'Exactly what is going on?'

All three slithered to a halt. Baxter looked them over, especially Zammo, still in his PE strip from the trials. Then his attention turned to Gripper.

'I hope you're not trying to do what I think you are, Stebson?' Gripper didn't answer, so Baxter turned to Jonah.

'He bothering you, lad?'

Jonah looked at Zammo, then at Gripper, who was standing quite nonchalantly watching the proceedings on the playing fields, apparently unconcerned by Baxter's intervention. Jonah knew what to expect if he said the wrong thing, so he remained silent. That was proof enough for Baxter. He turned to Zammo and Jonah.

'All right. You. Get yourself inside and get changed. You go with him.' He then turned to Gripper. 'You. Disappear.' Gripper hesitated. 'Now!'

Even Gripper knew you could only push Baxter so far, so he took a long hard look at Jonah and sloped off. As they went into the gym, they knew he would be waiting for them later. 'We're going to have to do something, Jonah. Or he'll kill us,' Zammo was saying as he rubbed his hair with his towel.

'I'm trying to think, aren't I?'

'Even if we sneak past him tonight, he'll still come

26

after us tomorrow. Or the next day. Or the day after. He's a mental case.'

'I bet he wouldn't even take extra money now, either,' Jonah said morosely.

'I'm not giving him nothing,' Zammo retorted.

'I'm not saying we should. All I'm saying is that he'll be so worked up, he wouldn't, even if we did.'

'So we've got to do something, haven't we?' Zammo repeated.

'Yeah . . . but what? He still outnumbers the two of us.'

Zammo was pulling on his pants as Baxter came in and dumped the nets and poles they'd put up around the hammer throwers.

'Hurry up, you two. You're the last ones here.'

As he went out, Zammo picked up one of the poles.

'We could crack him one with one of these.'

'If you got close enough to use it. And if he stood still long enough.'

Zammo nodded, throwing the pole back in despair and turning to put on his shoes and socks.

'We'd have to tie him down, or something,' Jonah continued.

'But even that'd take a small army. What are we going to do?' Zammo was beginning to sound a bit desperate. But he didn't get an answer. Jonah was on his feet and crossing to look at the nets Baxter had dumped.

'Jonah, I said what are we going to do?'

'Use this!' Jonah suddenly announced.

'What?'

'Use this. Throw it over him so he can't move.'

'You're mad.'

'No, I'm not. It's our only chance.'

27

'But . . . but what good will it do?' Zammo stammered. 'And . . . and . . . how are we going to get that out?'

'Simple,' announced Jonah, as he scooped up one of the nets, crossed to the window, opened it and dropped it outside. 'Like that!' He closed the window and crossed back to Zammo, just as Baxter came in.

'Come on, I want to lock up. I've got a home to go to, even if you haven't. Come on. Chop chop.'

Jonah moved to the door. Zammo followed, putting on his jacket and still a bit bemused by Jonah's idea. Baxter was in too much of a hurry to get home to notice that one of his nets was missing. He closed the door and turned the key.

Sure enough, Gripper was propping up a lamp post outside the main gates, as Jonah's head appeared above the fence just to the right of the gate. He ducked down beside Zammo, now carrying the net.

'This is crazy,' Zammo whispered.

'Not as crazy as him,' Jonah replied. 'Ready?'

Zammo swallowed and nodded. 'Nothing to lose, I suppose.'

Jonah grinned as he stood up, took hold of one end of the net and pulled it straight. He then laid his end on the ground, nodded at Zammo and moved towards the gate.

'Hey, pig features!'

Gripper was still leaning against the lamp post, watching a couple of Brookdale girls go by, as Jonah's voice suddenly called out from the gate.

'Hey, pig features! Want to try your . . .'

But he didn't finish as Gripper sprang towards him.

Jonah turned back inside the gate, and ran to his end of the net. 'Now!' he shouted. And he and Zammo ran towards the gate, so that as Gripper came dashing in after Jonah, he ran straight into the net. Jonah kicked at his feet until he fell over and Zammo rolled him over and over until he was quite definitely trapped.

'What the . . . you little . . . just wait till I . . .' Gripper kicked and tossed and cursed. But the more he struggled the more he tangled the net until he realized it was useless and finally gave up. Not until he was quite still did Jonah and Zammo step close.

'I'll get you for this,' Gripper spat at them.

'Cut it out, Gripper. Or we'll leave you in there,' Jonah said quickly.

'Yeah. Do you want to get out? Or stay there all night? Everyone else has gone home, you know.'

Gripper did know. 'Let me out, I said.'

'On one condition,' Jonah suggested.

'What?'

'You leave us alone!'

'Forever,' Zammo added. 'Now and in the future.'

'You won't have a future if you don't let me out, sunshine.'

'Come on, Zammo. Let's leave him then,' Jonah said as he pulled Zammo away. 'We'll just have to take our chances.' They started to walk away. They were both holding their breath, knowing it was a gamble, as they turned out of the gate.

Would he lose face too much? Would he rather stay there all night than give in to them? If he didn't he'd really be out for their blood. They were going down the street before they heard Gripper shout, 'All right!' They broke into huge grins and hurried back.

'You promise not to bother us?'

'Yeah . . .'

'Promise!'

'Yeah. Promise. Get me out.' Gripper didn't relish the idea of being left alone overnight.

Jonah exchanged a look with Zammo. Could they trust him? Zammo shrugged. After all, they had no other option. Jonah bent over Gripper and slowly rolled him over as Zammo pulled the net free, but not all the way. They didn't trust him that much. When it was clear that he could get out himself with a bit of time, they moved away towards the gate.

'You promised, Gripper,' Zammo reminded him.

'And we could always do it again, remember,' Jonah added, but then turned and ran as Gripper struggled free.

'Promised did I?' Gripper muttered as he tore the net aside. 'We'll see about that tomorrow.'

The next day Jonah and Zammo were on edge all day. Everywhere they went, they were expecting Gripper to appear any moment. One of them was always watching their backs as they moved about the school, but they saw neither sight nor sound of him.

'Reckon he's going to keep his promise?' Zammo asked as they left the school, but instead of an answer from Jonah he received one of a different, but equally clear sort.

The net they had used on Gripper was suddenly dropped over them and they stumbled and fell in a tangled mass. Then they saw the familiar DM's.

'All right, boys? Had a good day, have you?'

Gripper's voice drifted down as one of the DM's pulled back and then came flying towards each of them in turn.

'King Gripper never forgets a good laugh.' The DM's did their work once more, but then quite suddenly turned and walked away. It took Jonah and Zammo a good fifteen minutes to untangle themselves. There was no sign of Gripper. In fact they saw nothing more of him again until long after their bruised ribs had healed. He'd decided to leave them alone and seek easier prey – of which there was plenty around Grange Hill.

So their desperate gamble had paid off. Not so for Roland Browning, who was soon to become the centre of Gripper's attention.

It's All in the Mind

Roland Browning had never been thin. Not even as a baby. His mum had told him he was a big baby. Ten pounds, he thought she said, and not skinny and wrinkly like most babies, but quite chubby. Bonny, that's what he'd been called. A bonny, bouncing baby. As he grew up he remained bonny until he went to school.

There things soon changed. From the first day at Ladygrove Infants he ceased being bonny and became tubby.

As he progressed through life so his physical appearance grew. By the time he reached Grange Hill he had gone from tubby to blubber, bubble, fatty, fatso and now to Roly-Poly. What Roland couldn't figure out, was why people had to make an issue out of it. Why pick on him? Still, in more confident moments, which were becoming fewer, he realized it wasn't just him they picked on, but anyone who was different in any way, shape or form. Four eyes; lanky; shorty; rake; stump (for a boy with only one leg); chinky; paki; wog and so on and so on. Once you were identified as a target that was it.

The teasing, baiting, and bullying went on and on, making your life one long misery. For Roland, life at

Grange Hill was becoming unbearable, especially since he had come under the close scrutiny of that apprentice Mafia Don, Gripper Stebson.

Unfortunately for Roland, he was an obvious target. Not simply because of his size and appearance, but because of his subservient attitude. He would never stand up for himself, or ever try to fight back. If anyone demanded money he would pay up. If they demanded his lunch he would give it. It wasn't his fault he was timid.

A lot of people are. And why should he risk being beaten up every day? Perhaps that fear had made him the way he was. Roland had often heard about people eating because they are unhappy. The more unhappy they are, the more they eat. The more they eat, the fatter they become. The fatter they become, the more problems they have and the more unhappy they become. And so it goes on. Was he timid because he was fat? Or was he fat because he was timid?

Roland thought about this as he waddled along towards school. Perhaps I should go on another diet, he mused, as he broke off the end of a chocolate cream bar and devoured half in one easy chomp. Never works though, I always get too hungry. Perhaps I'm naturally like this. Why should I change? Perhaps I've got a rare disease like people get when they're trying to stay thin. Wonder if I should get Mum to take me to the doctor's. Mind you, she reckons I'll grow out of it, doesn't she? And Dad. He reckons it's puppy fat. He looked down at his stomach, forcing its way out between the two sides of his blazer.

Wonder when, though?

He turned into the gate and was just about to polish off the mint cream when a hand closed around it.

'Hang about, Roly. Haven't I warned you that too many sweets are bad for you?' Roland froze. It was Gripper. He had a couple of mates with him today so it was doubly dangerous. They weren't really mates. No one could be mates with Gripper, but some people felt it was safer to knock about with him because at least then you always knew where he was. It was safer for them but more dangerous for everyone else. Gripper would be out to impress, as well as remind them how vicious he could be. Roland could see it was the latter this morning.

'Right lads,' Gripper continued, twisting Roland's ear with his other hand. 'You know what too many sweets does to you, Roly? It makes you fat!' He poked Roland in the stomach to the great delight of the others. Most people were just relieved that it was Roland on the receiving end – and not them. 'Now what have I taught you since you've been here?' Gripper squeezed his ear. 'What do you do in the presence of King Gripper?'

Roland knew and slowly sank to his knees. Gripper laughed, turned to receive the admiration of his followers, but then screwed up his own face in pain as someone else grabbed his ear.

It was Tucker Jenkins. 'And what do you do in the presence of Emperor Tucker, Stebson my old mate?'

The first thing Gripper did was release Roland's ear. The second thing he did he regretted. He tried to take a kick at Tucker, but of course Tucker had been around a long time. He was standing too far back, and as he sidestepped the flailing DM, Tucker calmly kicked Gripper's other leg from under him and he collapsed in a heap on the ground. Where were Gripper's henchmen now? Standing back taking it all in. None of them wanted to get involved. Not with Tucker, and definitely not with Tucker's constant shadow, big Alan Humphries. No one argues with or tries to bully him, Roland thought, as he watched Stebson's cronies slowly melt away. It wasn't just the fact that Alan belonged to the judo club that intimidated people. Roland knew it was also his size. He was almost as fat as himself. But he used his size as an asset, not a handicap. Roland knew it was difficult arguing with twelve stone of angry fat. If Alan ever sat on someone he'd soon get his own way, Roland knew. He'd seen Alan Humphries in action. But Alan appeared to have one thing Roland didn't: confidence. Then there was Tucker Jenkins, he had confidence. He always seemed ready and willing to take on anyone, whether pupil or staff. Right now he was giving Gripper a bad time and as Roland got to his feet he was grateful for the fact.

'When you going to learn to pick on someone your own size, Stebson?'

'He's miles bigger than me, isn't he?' Stebson sneered.

'Why don't you try the same on me then?' Alan asked, standing on Stebson's hand.

'Gerroff . . .' He was about to say *fatso*, but thought better of it. Gripper had been in this situation before, both sides, although usually he would be handing out the treatment. The sooner you co-operated, the sooner it was over. It was one of the basic rules of survival. So he held his tongue and waited for the next move, which would be to make him apologize.

'Haven't heard you say you're sorry to Slim-Jim, here,' Tucker said. Stebson grinned at guessing right, while Roland groaned inwardly. Even his rescuers ridiculed him.

'Come on, then,' Tucker prompted by bending

forward and pulling Stebson to his feet by his hair. 'You owe him an apology, don't you?'

'Stuff it!' He couldn't bring himself to do it. Alan suddenly had his right arm twisted across his back and under his left armpit.

'Didn't quite catch that,' Tucker said.

'I said . . . stuff . . . arrgggghhh!' Alan had his arm practically wrapped around his body. 'O.K. O.K.!'

Alan let go. Stebson rubbed his shoulder, feeling sure Alan had dislocated it. One of these days, he thought, as he glared at Alan.

'Don't even think it, Stebson. I'd chew you up before breakfast,' said Alan.

'We're still waiting,' Tucker reminded him.

'I'm sorry, blubber. O.K.?'

Tucker's hand shot out and caught Stebson across the temple. 'Do it properly.'

Stebson snarled, but knew he'd never get away otherwise. 'I'm sorry. Right?'

Tucker turned to Roland. 'You willing to accept that apology?' Roland nodded quickly. He wanted to get it over. The last thing he wanted to do was give Gripper another excuse to pick on him.

'On your way, creep,' said Alan pushing Stebson away.

'Oh, and don't get any funny ideas like jumping him later. Clear?' said Tucker.

Stebson didn't reply but just gave a finger sign to Alan, who took one step, causing Stebson to run. At last he'd gone. Roland felt relieved, but not for long.

'After your mint cream, was he?' Tucker asked.

Roland nodded and showed them the bar. Which was a mistake. Tucker immediately took it, broke off one piece, gave it back and split the rest between himself and Alan. 'One thing he was right about, Roly. Too many of these make you fat.'

With that he winked and sauntered off. Alan followed. Roland looked down at his remaining piece of mint cream. Typical, that is, he thought as he set off for registration. Even people who come to help you rip you off. Still, at least I've got a bit – which is more than I'd have got off Gripper. *And* I didn't have to hand over any cash. He looked back across the playground to see Tucker and Alan talking to a group of girls. Wonder why they did it, he thought. Probably more interested in the aggro than me. He shrugged and turned into the main teaching block.

He walked along the main corridor and started the long haul up to the form room for registration. Why does it have to be at the top, he moaned to himself as he dragged his bulk up the stairs. Then his mind moved back to Alan Humphries. Wonder if he has trouble climbing stairs? Probably fitter than me if he does judo.

Roland stopped for breath on the second landing. He's definitely more confident than I am, his thoughts continued. He's even got a girlfriend. She does judo too. I wonder if that's it. Because he's good at judo. Could be. No one can knock him about, can they? Must have something to do with it. I wouldn't be afraid of Gripper if I knew judo, would I? I bet it's because he's good at judo. Or just good at something. Perhaps I should give it a try. Join the club. Learn how to do it. How to throw my weight about. He chuckled at this unintentional pun, but that was how the idea came to him. Between the second and third floor landings. Roland decided he would take up judo.

But like most things Roland tried to do, he found it full of disappointment.

'Sorry, lad. You're just not fit enough. Even if there was a place available. Which there isn't,' Mr Baxter, the head of sport, informed him when he went to make enquiries.

'But I want to learn how to defend myself, sir.'

'No doubt you do. But the first thing you want to do is work off some of that weight. Get half of that off and you won't need to defend yourself. Even if you do you'll be able to run twice as fast to keep out of trouble.' Baxter smiled and walked away, leaving Roland feeling very deflated. Why didn't anything ever go right for him? He just couldn't understand it. Just as he couldn't understand how he'd found his way down to the shopping precinct and was now on his way back to school just polishing off half-a-pound of liquorice torpedoes. He stopped walking so suddenly that an old lady following him bumped into his back.

'Look out. Watch where you're going, will you!' she muttered as she shoved him aside. Why did little old ladies always think they had the right to push and shove people about? If anyone should have watched where they were going it was her, thought Roland as he turned his attention back to the sweet bag, now with only two torpedoes left. How did I eat them all, he wondered. And why did I do it anyway? It must be right. That bit about fat people eating to console themselves. I'm doing it without noticing.

He screwed up the bag and threw it across the precinct. As he did he heard a voice from behind.

'Oi. What do you think you're up to?' Roland turned to see one of the precinct security men looking across. 'Pick it up and put it in the bin. Council spends enough trying to keep this place decent.'

Huh, not that I'd noticed, Roland thought as he

41

picked up the sweet bag. Even his gesture of despair had caused him more trouble. He walked over to the rubbish bin and dropped the bag inside, though he unfolded the bag, took out the two remaining torpedoes and popped them into his mouth before he did so.

He started back to school as depressed as ever.

It was Miss Mooney who noticed how miserable he looked. It was always Miss Mooney. She seemed to be the only one who cared. Everyone thought she was a bit loopy, but at least she was always concerned about them. Like the time she stopped Mr Curtis giving Zammo and Jonah the cane. Roland had admired her for that. Took a bit of guts that did, standing up to Curtis. Almost as much as it'd take for him to stand up to Gripper. Yes, Roland liked Miss Mooney, even if she was a bit scatter-brained.

'Could you stay behind please, Roland,' Miss Mooney said as she dismissed them all after registration. By the time Roland had squeezed out of his desk and down to the front, the room was practically deserted.

'Close the door please, Annette,' Miss Mooney told her as Annette left. As usual she was hanging back trying to find out what was going on. Nosy cow!

'Well, Roland. And what's wrong today?'

'Nothing, miss.'

'Oh, come along. I've known you long enough.'

'It's nothing, miss. Honest.'

'Has that horrid boy ... er ... Stebson been pestering you again?'

'Er ... no, miss.' But his hesitation and sideways glance gave him away.

'I see ... What was it this time?'

'Nothing. It was nothing, miss. He did try, miss, but
. . . well . . . that Tucker Jenkins and Alan Humphries
sorted him out for me.'

'For you? Interested in a fight more like.'

'Still helped me, miss.'

'Ye-es. I suppose so.' She didn't sound too happy
about it.

'What was it about?'

Roland shrugged. 'You know. Usual. And he tried
to steal my sweets.'

'Oh, you're not still eating sweets.'

'Yes, miss,' Roland said quietly, an amazingly guilty
look on his face.

'I thought we agreed you would try and give them
up?' She was right. They had. Well, she had, the last
time they had this sort of talk and he told her how
unhappy he was about being so fat. And he had
promised, as she now reminded him.

'Yeah . . . but it's so hard, miss,' he complained.
'Sometimes I eat them without even knowing it.'

'Nonsense!'

'No . . . I do, miss. I did it at lunchtime. I was so busy
thinking about Gripper and that, that I'd eaten a whole
bag. And I couldn't even remember buying . . .' he
trailed off as he suddenly felt his throat tighten and
tears forming in his eyes. He swallowed to try and clear
his throat and quickly wiped the back of his hand
across his eyes.

'All right. There's no need to upset yourself, Roland.
We're all a bit absent-minded at times, aren't we . . .
even I am, you know.'

You don't have to tell me, he was thinking when he
looked up to see the smile on her face. She was making
fun of herself as she was the most absent-minded

43

person in the school; the whole school knew it and obviously so did she. It managed to squeeze a smile out of Roland.

'We all do things, or have things about us, that we don't like, now don't we?' Roland nodded.

That seemed like fair comment. Miss Mooney continued, 'Some things we can do something about. Others we can't. So we have to learn to live with it. I've got a terrible memory so I had to learn to write things down. But knowing it makes me uncertain. Nervous. Jumpy. I get flustered so I can't concentrate. So I can't find my notes.' Miss Mooney raised her eyes and smiled. 'It's like a vicious circle, isn't it?'

Roland nodded again. He understood exactly what she was saying. 'I know that, miss. But it's just . . .' He shrugged, not quite knowing how to put it into words.

'It's what, Roland?'

'Well . . . it's er . . . you know. It's just different being fat, isn't it?'

'Why?'

'Everyone can see your problem. Even if you want to do something about it, it takes so long, doesn't it?'

'You mean lose weight?'

'Ye-ah. You still have to put up with the aggro even while you're doing it. And it, you know, gets to you so you feel miserable all the time and then well, you know.' He trailed off again with another shrug.

'And then you eat?'

'Yeah.'

It was now Miss Mooney's turn to nod. She understood exactly what Roland was saying. She was also very surprised at how forthcoming Roland had been. Usually she would have had to prise most of the

44

information out of him. She realized he must have been thinking about it quite seriously. She looked at her watch. They were both five minutes late for their next period. She couldn't keep her next class waiting.

'Look, Roland. Time's pressing on. Can we continue this later?'

'Suppose so, miss,' Roland answered, sounding a lot less than enthusiastic. They turned towards the door.

'It's all a matter of self-confidence, really. If you've got that, it shouldn't matter how you look or act.'

'But how do you get that way?'

'Er, I'm afraid I don't know. I suppose, well, I suppose it's being good at something. Having a skill or a talent.'

'Count me out then.'

'Oh, don't sound so negative all the time. There must be something you're good at.'

'Oh yeah,' Roland replied as they left the room.

'Oh . . . what?' Miss Mooney enquired eagerly.

'Eating!' Roland said, then walked away towards the stairs.

Miss Mooney let out a long sigh, and went in the opposite direction. She could see real problems ahead with Roland. However, their chat had made some impression on Roland, if only because she had taken the time to talk to him. The rest of the afternoon he spent thinking about what she had said about self-confidence. He had looked around and saw Jonah, Zammo, Annette, Fay and all the others. All seemed to have it. Why didn't he? Because he was fat? What about Alan Humphries? Was it just his judo? He'd read something about him in one of the school magazines. The article was about the judo club but it said something about his being a chess champion. Or good at chess. Something like that. Roland wondered if that had anything to do with it as well. There should be *something* I'm good at, he thought. But what? That was the question. To which the answer appeared: nothing. It was true that he was good at guessing the weight of the fruit and veg in the shop where his mum worked. In fact he quite liked helping out every now and then, but a talent for knowing how many spuds, or how many tomatoes, or how many mushrooms weighed a kilo would hardly be big news at Grange Hill.

Just as he had decided for the twentieth time that he was absolutely useless, Roland realized someone was trying to communicate with him. It was quite a soft voice, whispering so as not to be overheard. As it slowly seeped into his consciousness, Roland recognized it as belonging to Jonah.

'Oi, deaf lugs. I'm talking to you!' Jonah poked him on the shoulder, keeping an eye on Mrs Gordon, their Geography teacher, who was drawing a map on the board.

Roland turned. 'What?'

'What's that you got in your hand?' Roland didn't know what Jonah was talking about, so deep had he been in his own thoughts.

'In your hands, dimbo,' Jonah repeated, raising his eyes as though Roland was an idiot.

Roland looked down to see a miniature paper aeroplane. How had it got there? He must have made it because it was a design he had made up himself. He tended to do that sort of thing during games when he was left alone in the changing room.

Actually he was quite proud of this particular design. It had both wings, tail fin and rear stabilizers all folded

from the one piece. It had taken him five or six full
games periods to perfect, but it flew for about ten
metres if launched properly. He called it the Browning
Bomber. But he couldn't remember making this
particular model.

'Let's see it then?' Jonah whispered.

As Roland passed it over he realized it was made
from another chocolate bar wrapping. He closed his
eyes and sighed. He must have made it while he was
thinking about his chat with Miss Mooney. It could
mean only one thing. He had been eating again. His
next thought was the obvious one. As soon as Jonah
examined the paper aeroplane he would also recognize
the wrapper and demand a piece of chocolate. Rather
then face the hassle, Roland dug into his pockets to find
the bar, but then stopped when he realized he had
guessed wrong. He was even more surprised to hear
Zammo lean over and whisper: 'It's rocket this, Roly.
Could you make us one?'

Roland half-turned in his chair. Had he heard
right?

'How'd you make it?' Jonah was asking.

Roland looked at them, then at the plane. They
seemed genuinely interested.

'How'd you get the tail bit on as well?' Zammo
wanted to know. He started to unfold the plane, but
Jonah thumped him.

'Don't knacker it. Must have taken Roly ages to
make that.'

'Oh . . . yeah. Sorry, Roly.'

Roland couldn't believe this. Jonah actually protect-
ing him. The only other time he had shown any interest
was to ask him to help dump snow over Annette
Firman. The same applied to Zammo. His only real

47

interest was when he had scrounged some lunch and a pullover when Jonah fell in the sea lion pool when they all went to the zoo.

Still, despite this rather dubious and self-centred past record they did look genuinely impressed by the Browning Bomber.

'Did it take yonks?' Jonah asked again.

'Not really,' Roland said, trying to sound as casual as possible.

'How far'll it fly?'

'About ten metres.'

Jonah let out a slow whistle through his teeth, being careful not to let Mrs Gordon hear. He was impressed. So much so he turned round to the desks behind.

'Pssstt . . . Bagsey . . . Take a squint at this.'

He passed the plane over, and it was received with the same respect as it passed from person to person. Even Annette Firman, the only girl in the form to take an interest, seemed quite impressed.

Before long, news of Roland's plane had swept the first three years. Soon squadrons of Browning Bombers were floating, swooping and diving through the Grange Hill skies. Roland had become something of a celebrity, as the man who started the micro-plane craze.

By half-term, his whole attitude to life had changed. He had found something everyone else thought he was good at. Without realizing it, he had gradually come to feel more confident. But what pleased Roland even more was that his desire to eat all the time had gone. He still ate more than anyone else, but by his own standards he was on a diet. Life began to seem worth living after all.

Then, one day, halfway between Maths and French, he felt a tap on the shoulder, and that old familiar voice. King Gripper.

'Oi . . . Roly. Give us a sweet.'

'I er . . . I haven't got any, Gripper.' He squawked as his ear was gripped. 'Owwww . . . I mean King Gripper.'

'Why haven't you got any? Lump of lard like you always has sweets.'

'I don't eat them any more.'

'Don't you? Well I do. You have some by tomorrow or . . .' He demonstrated what would happen on Roland's ear, then sauntered off.

Roland stood rubbing his ear. He used to get aggro because he was always eating sweets. And now he was getting it because he didn't. He let out a long sigh and carried on his way, muttering to himself.

'You just can't win, in this place.'

Boys Will Be Boys and Girls Will Be . . .?

Annette Firman was a tomboy. At least that's what everyone always said. Ever since she could remember, people had used the phrase about her. Especially her Auntie Luke. She was the first one Annette could remember using it and so Annette blamed her for it. She just couldn't understand why everyone made such a fuss about it. She liked to play with boys. But that was because she liked to climb trees, throw stones, mess about with her dad's car and a hundred other things that only boys are supposed to do. But she also liked pretty dresses, cosmetics, dolls – girls' things. Annette liked doing anything, so long as she had a good laugh. Why should that make her a tomboy? She hated the description. Just as she hated her Auntie Luke.

Well, perhaps hate was too strong a term for it, but she definitely thought that she was loopy. Even her name was ridiculous. How could an Auntie be called Luke? Annette knew it was because her name was really Lucinda, but why didn't she call herself Lucy? And if anyone was a tomboy it was Auntie Luke. Annette always thought she was a bit odd, but it wasn't her Auntie Luke she was thinking about this morning, as she trudged her way to Grange Hill. Annette wasn't thinking of anything or anyone in particular, but

53

about the thin layer of snow that had fallen overnight.

'Hey, Annette!' someone called, and she turned to see it was Fay Lucas, trying to hurry to catch up with her, but slightly nervous of slipping over. She had Belinda Zowkowski with her. Annette rated Belinda not much higher than Auntie Luke, considering her as wet as the snow on the ground.

'Hi,' she said to Fay. She decided to ignore Belinda.

'This is brilliant, isn't it?' Fay said as she scooped up a handful, made a snowball and threw it across the road at a road sign. She missed.

'Yeah,' Annette agreed, quite excited. She was thinking more about what they could get up to later.

'It's nothing special,' droned Belinda. 'Back home in Canada we get twenty feet of snow. You can't go out a lot of the time.' Here she goes again, thought Annette. Canada this. Canada that. Right pain in the bum she is about Canada. Wish she'd bloomin' well stopped there.

'Reckon it'll stick?' Fay asked, unaware of Annette's irritation. 'Never usually does, does it?'

'Stick long enough for us to have a laugh. If we don't hang about all day going on about all our yesterdays.'

'What?' Fay asked, not understanding, but Annette had set off towards the gate. Fay looked at Belinda, who just shrugged.

'Probably something to do with me,' she offered.

'What makes you say that?'

'She's never been very friendly towards me.'

'She's never been very friendly towards anyone. C'mon.'

She hurried, as best she could, after Annette. Belinda let out a long sigh and tagged along. She knew she was tagging along because she always did. She always had.

54

Although she was born in Canada, her father worked for a large multi-national company and he was always being transferred from country to country. No sooner had she settled down and made friends than the family was on the move again. She never had time to make any lasting friendships, so she just tagged along.

By the time Belinda had caught up with the others, Annette was demonstrating how she, like it or not, earned her tomboy image. The person selected for this demonstration, although he was still completely unaware of the fact, was the fat boy of N1, Roland Browning. Poor old Roland. Not only did he have to contend with his size, but his very shape made him an obvious and easy target for the likes of Gripper Stebson, who was rapidly taking over the role left empty when that arch nutjob Booga Benson was expelled for putting Tucker Jenkins in hospital. Roland was doing his best to stay upright on the snow by leaning against the school fence as he approached.

Naturally, this rather timid and precarious method of travel attracted a few eyes, including Annette's. She was now finding it almost too difficult to contain her excitement at the prospect of pelting Roland from a mound of snowballs she and Fay had prepared.

'Don't be so horrible,' Belinda protested when she saw what they were planning. 'You're always picking on him.'

'Saves me picking on you then, doesn't it?' Annette sneered and then nudged Fay as Roland came into sight, clutching the gatepost to retain his balance.

Belinda felt like warning Roland, but she couldn't find enough nerve, knowing if she did she would become Annette's next target. Instead she decided not to watch and walked away. 'You are horrible, you know.' The only reply she received was a snowball sailing past her head. She sighed and walked on into the school. 'Hey, Roland!' Annette called, her voice now squeaky with expectation. 'Catch!'

As Roland looked up to see who was calling him, both Annette and Fay let fly a salvo of snowballs. Instinctively, he let go of the gatepost to cover his head with his hands, and lost his balance. His legs flew out in front of him and he came down on his backside with a resounding thump. Annette exploded with shrieks of laughter. As Roland dropped out of the line of fire, Annette's two sworn enemies, Jonah and Zammo, came through the gate and straight into the line of fire.

'What the . . .' Jonah exclaimed as he took one snowball straight in the chest and another on the side of his head. As it shattered against his ear, Zammo took the full force of the fallout as well as a glancing blow to his knee from another.

'Firman!' Zammo shouted as he nudged Jonah and pointed, but by this time the girls had turned and fled.

'Bloomin' 'eck, went right down me neck that did,' Jonah moaned as he bent forward and tried to shake out the residue from his collar.

'Same here. But it's better than what old Roly got by the looks of it.'

Jonah turned to see Roland standing up, but pulling his trousers away from his backside. Where he had fallen was right where everyone came in, and consequently the snow had been churned into slush. His trousers were soaked through. 'Been wetting yourself again, Roly?' Jonah tried to joke. Roland obviously didn't think it was funny. He turned and wobbled off to find a radiator. Someone his size and shape had to put up with such incidents – but not Jonah and Zammo.

'We can get her at break,' Zammo suggested.

'It'll be a wet break. They won't let us out.'

'Dinner time then.'

Jonah looked up at the sun, just managing to push a few rays through a heavily overcast sky.

'It might have gone then. If those clouds go away.'

'Doesn't look much chance of that.'

'No one thought it would snow last night did they?' Jonah now straightened up, having scooped out most of the snow.

'First time in fifteen years or something, it's been like this.'

'Says who?'

'It was on the radio this morning.'

'First time it's snowed?' Jonah didn't sound too convinced.

'Nah . . . first time it's stuck. Look out, here's Gripper.'

Jonah turned to see Gripper Stebson come through the gate, grab a first year and push him over in the snow, rolling him over and over until, like Roland, he was soaked.

'Let's go,' Jonah said. Zammo didn't need to be asked twice.

By this time Annette and Fay had reached the main teaching block and were about to go in for registration. 'His face was brilliant, wasn't it?' Fay laughed, thinking about Jonah.

'Serves him right,' Annette replied, as she bent down to form another snowball and carried it into the building.

'What are you up to now?'

'Might have gone by lunchtime, mightn't it?'

'So what are you going to do with that?'

'You'll see.' Annette grinned. Fay followed, curious. She didn't have to wait long. In fact only as long as it took to reach the second floor on the stairway that led up to their form room.

Instead of turning off towards registration, Annette stepped back to the railings and peered down the stairwell so she could watch everyone coming up.

'What are you doing?'

'Waiting.'

'For what?'

'You'll see.'

A few minutes later, Jonah and Zammo came up the stairs. They were chatting away to each other when Annette's voice boomed down from above. 'Hey, Jones!' Not thinking, Jonah looked up . . . and took the force of Annette's snowball full in the face. Zammo once again took the secondary fallout.

This time Jonah was quick to react. He was halfway up the next flight of stairs before Zammo had realized what had happened. Once he did, he charged after Jonah – who was now right behind Annette as she reached their form room. Belinda found herself shoved against Miss Mooney's desk as Annette scrambled through a group gathered round the front desks, pulling chairs over behind her in an attempt to trip or slow down Jonah. However, Jonah came crashing through the door after her, almost tripped over Belinda as she bounced off Miss Mooney's desk, but then leaped up on to the desks and pursued Annette at desk top height. It was on their second full circuit of the room, Annette dodging between the desks and Jonah jumping across them that Miss Mooney walked in.

'Gordon Jones, what on earth do you think you are doing?'

'He's chasing me, miss.' Annette was quick to try and act the innocent party, which was something of an art she had developed.

'I can see that, Annette, but why?'

'She threw a snowball at me, miss.'

'It was only a little snowball, miss.'

But Miss Mooney wasn't listening. Roland had just waddled in and she noticed his wet clothes.

'Roland, what on earth?'

'I er . . . fell over in the snow, miss.'

Miss Mooney let out a long sigh.

'Well, really! This is too much.' Miss Mooney's face was red with exasperation. 'Good heavens, I don't know what's the matter with you all. A little bit of snow and you all start acting like babies. Although I should have expected it from you, Jones. I don't know how many times I've had to speak to you about trivial, silly, childish little things. Get down off that desk!'

Jonah climbed down. 'She threw a snowball at me, miss.'

'I don't care. If you aren't man enough to take that sort of thing by now . . . Oh, I don't know. Get outside. I'll deal with you later.'

'But miss, she threw it when I was . . .'

'I don't care how or when she threw it. Get out.'

Jonah sighed. He knew it was hopeless arguing and it would only make matters worse. He did not bother to look across at Annette as he knew she'd have that stupid smirk on her face. How does she get away with it, he wondered. Zammo must have realized what he was thinking as he gave a sympathetic shrug as Jonah left, then moved across to sit down, making sure he passed Annette on the way. 'You'll get yours after,' he hissed.

'It'll be gone by then,' Annette smirked as she went to sit down. 'Or can't you see the sun?'

Zammo turned. She was right. The clouds had started to clear already. The snow would be gone by lunchtime. He sat down as Miss Mooney told Roland to go home and change. She couldn't possibly let him stay like that.

As Roland left, Jonah was too busy looking through the corridor window up at the sky. He too had noticed the sky clearing. It looked as though he wouldn't be able to get his revenge with the snow. Typical that, Jonah thought, I quite fancied the idea of stuffing it down her neck. Just have to think of something else I suppose, because she's not going to get away with it. I'll wipe that stupid smirk off her face.

He turned away from the window, walked back and had a look through the glass panel in the door. The first person he saw was Annette, looking directly at him. She still had that smirk on her face, then with a quick glance to see if Miss Mooney was watching, she stuck out her tongue at Jonah.

He turned away and went back to the window, clenching and unclenching his fists. I've got to get her somehow, he said to himself as he took another look at the sky. It was getting brighter by the second. That's that then, he thought and once again turned away. As he did, something caught his eye down in the playground. What is it? He nipped across to the door. Miss Mooney had just started the register. He looked at his watch. Take her at least five minutes; couple more for notices and that. His mind was beginning to click into gear. Gives me about eight minutes. I wonder if I could. He crossed to the window. Another look down at the playground, then at his watch. It's now or never, he thought. Then he turned and dashed towards the stairs.

When Miss Mooney finished the register she moved on, as Jonah expected, to read a couple of notices. The first was what they had all expected, that today would be a wet break. The remainder were reminders about the forthcoming School Play, a Jumble Sale, and about getting their deposits in for the school holiday. By the time she had made an appeal for the latest world disaster victims, everyone was beginning to pack up and move off to History, considered only slightly less boring than Miss Mooney's constant appeals to remember those children less fortunate than themselves. Still, someone had to do it and she always managed to scrape up a few pounds. Trouble was these days that there were too many good causes on the scrounge. At least that's what Zammo thought as he headed towards the door.

'Oh, McGuire. Ask Jones to come in, would you?' Miss Mooney asked as he opened the door. 'And Annette. You stay behind too, please.'

The request came as a bit of a shock to Annette, and for once she wasn't smirking. Belinda couldn't resist a small one, though. Outside, Zammo was puzzled to see no sign of Jonah. He was beginning to wonder if he'd decided to bunk off, and worrying about Miss Mooney coming out to look herself, when Jonah came up the stairs, struggling against the flow of the changeover tide. He was shaking his hands, blowing on them and tucking them under his arms as though they were freezing. They were. Which Zammo found out as Jonah grabbed his face between his hands.

'Watcha, Zammo.'

'Leave off! Where've you been?'

'Playground.'

'What for?'

'Felt like it.'

'What?'

'Tell you later. She want to see me?'

Zammo nodded, grinning. 'And she kept Attila the Nun back and all.'

Jonah grinned. 'What sort of mood she in now?'

Zammo shrugged. 'Same as before, I suppose.'

'Better get in there then, hadn't I.' He moved towards the door.

'Yeah . . . see you in History.'

Jonah pulled a face and went in to see Miss Mooney. Zammo looked out of the window at the sky. He tutted. Definitely missed our chance there, he thought as he turned away and joined the crush on the stairs.

Jonah and Annette each received an hour's detention.

Annette had protested her innocence, as usual, but Miss Mooney was in no mood to listen. In fact she had initially only given her half-an-hour for provoking Jonah, but her repeated protests earned her the extra half-hour. So it was Jonah who was smirking as Miss Mooney walked away to find her next class.

'Should have kept your mouth shut when you only had half-an-hour,' he teased. 'Although it must be difficult with one that big.'

'Huh, listen who's talking,' she replied, before adding, 'but at least I never got covered in snow.'

Her smirk returned as she began to walk away, stopping at the window. 'Pity it looks like it's melting, isn't it?'

'Yeah, it is,' muttered Jonah. And he too grinned as

he looked out of the window and then followed her down to History.

'It certainly is.'

The rest of the morning was fairly uneventful. They dozed through History. During break everyone stayed indoors and the snow rapidly disappeared in the morning sun. By the time Roland returned in dry clothes at eleven o'clock it had practically gone. By twelve-thirty all that was left were damp patches where the snow had been thickest.

Also by twelve-thirty Zammo had nagged Jonah into telling him what he had been up to. Jonah showed him.

'Rocket!' Zammo exclaimed. 'It's brill, Jonah. When are we going to do it?'

'Soon as we can find her,' Jonah replied and led Zammo away from the boiler house to hunt for Annette.

After half-an-hour they had no luck whatsoever. 'Thought she stayed for dinner.' Zammo flopped against a wall to take the weight off his legs.

'Mustn't do,' Jonah said, looking round the playground.

'Do you think we'll be able to manage it? By ourselves, I mean?' Zammo suddenly asked.

'Yeah. She's only a girl, isn't she?'

'Oh yeah. But she's stronger than half the blokes around here.'

Jonah nodded. That's true, he thought. She isn't a girl's girl, is she? Like that soppy Canadian. Sneeze on *her* and she'd fall over. And she has got that mate, Fay Lucas, hasn't she? He turned back to Zammo. 'Think we should get reinforcements, then?'

'Best had, I reckon. Don't want to blow it, do you? We'll probably only get one crack at it.'

Jonah nodded again. Zammo was right. But who? Who did they know well enough? Or who hated Firman badly enough? As these thoughts went through his mind he glanced around the playground again. And then he knew the answer. Through the maze of football matches, each playing across the other, and often confused as to whose ball was whose, their reinforcements came waddling into view.

'Oh, come on, Roland,' Zammo urged. 'She tried to do you this morning, didn't she?'

'Yes . . . but I don't want to fight with a girl,' Roland moaned.

'You won't be fighting with a girl,' Jonah said quickly.

'That's the whole idea. So there won't be a fight.'

Roland still looked unsure. 'I don't want to get detention either.'

'You won't. I promise you.'

'How? How can you do that?'

'By keeping a good look out.'

'Oh, come on, Roland,' Zammo started again. 'It's only a bit of a laugh, isn't it? And getting our own back. It's not as if we're doing it just for the aggro, is it? Like she done. Know what I mean?'

Roland did. He was constantly the victim of aggro and he still couldn't figure out why people had to pick on him. Or anyone else for that matter. But he had to admit he wanted to. She had always made fun of his size. 'You sure we won't be seen or anything? I don't want detention.'

'So you said,' Zammo said wearily.

Jonah nudged him. 'Course I am. I wouldn't do it otherwise, now would I? I'm not going to land myself in it, am I?' Jonah sounded so confident that Roland finally nodded.

While this was going on Annette and Fay had shaken off Belinda. Annette moaned about her always 'tagging along', as they were walking back to school after a visit to the local shopping precinct. They had been to look at the new Model Shop, where Fay had made the mistake of hinting that the stuff there was mostly for boys. All the way back Annette had been going on at her about there being no difference between boys and girls, until in the end she was becoming a pain. More and more irritated, Fay responded in a way she knew was equally annoying to Annette.

'But not all of us are tomboys like you, Annette.'

It had the desired effect. She was quiet for a good two minutes although Fay wasn't quite sure whether it was through anger or sheer exhaustion. Eventually, Annette spoke. 'That's a stupid phrase.'

She was trying to sound as nonchalant as possible, which was the reason for the lengthy pause, while she composed herself. The one thing she hated above being called a tomboy, was for people to know how much she hated it. But Fay had seen her react to it at home.

'It's what you are, though, isn't it?' Fay continued, deliberately baiting her. 'No matter what you call it. You're like that, aren't you? Like messing about like boys.'

'It's not like boys. It's just, just having a good laugh.'

'Like those snowballs this morning?'

'You joined in.'

'Only outside. I didn't throw any inside. That's what I mean. That's the sort of thing a boy would do.'

Annette just laughed, but Fay went on, 'I wouldn't

like to guess what Jones would have done to you if Miss Mooney hadn't come in.'

'Huh! He would've had to catch me first.'

'He nearly did.'

'So what? He wouldn't have done anything,' she said with scorn. 'I'm a girl, aren't I? And boys aren't supposed to hit girls. It's bad for their image.'

'Oh yeah? Well, I wouldn't push it too far if I was you.'

Annette laughed. 'Don't be stupid. It was just a good laugh. That's all it . . .'

She was about to continue when another voice joined the conversation.

'It's a good laugh you're looking for is it?' The two girls turned and were surprised to see Jonah, Zammo and Roland standing behind them. They were even more surprised to see they each had a handful of snowballs. It was Jonah who spoke first.

'You know what else is bad for a bloke's image, Firman? Letting a woman get the better of him. Ready lads?'

They were. Annette received a full broadside. She was covered from head to toe in snow, as at least a dozen snowballs exploded against her body, legs and head. Neither she nor Fay could figure out where they had got the snow from, but as Annette ducked into a doorway trying to find what shelter she could, Jonah unveiled his source of supply – and where he had been while Miss Mooney called registration: to fill one of the bins outside the boiler house full of snow. He had worked out that the snow inside the bin would survive the sun, although it was now only about a quarter full. The boys were scooping out handfuls to hurl at Annette. She was huddled in a corner, her back turned in an attempt to minimize her suffering. Fay was keeping well clear.

'Now!' shouted Jonah, as the three boys jumped forward. Roland dragged Annette from the doorway while Jonah and Zammo lifted the dustbin as high as they could and tipped out the remaining snow over Annette's head. Then they dropped the bin and beat a retreat.

'How's that for a good laugh?' called Jonah as they raced away across the playground.

'And how's that for being just like the boys?' Fay couldn't resist asking.

Annette didn't answer. She just spat out the snow, brushed it out of her hair and off her clothes as best she could – then walked away.

'Where you going?' Fay asked.

'To change,' Annette replied.

But from the look in her eye, she was also going to plan her revenge. She might have lost this time, but – you can't keep a good tomboy down.

Appreciation

Tucker hated English. Not that that was too surprising. Tucker hated most subjects. In fact he hated almost everything to do with school. Well, not quite everything. He liked the practical subjects, and Art. He enjoyed making things. But reading old books? He could never see the point. 'I hate this rubbish,' he whispered to Tommy, who was busy reading *Penthouse* under the desk.

'What?'

'This garbage. Why do they bother trying to make us read it? I mean, I can't see the point of having to be taught how to appreciate something, can you?'

'Nah . . . I can appreciate that though.' Tommy grinned, showing him one of the pictures. Tucker just tutted and raised his eyes. He couldn't see the point of drooling over a stupid magazine either. He looked round the room. The only person who seemed to be paying any attention was Sooty. And that was probably only because he was paid to.

Doyle was scratching his initials into the desk lid, again. Benny was gazing out of the window, probably dreaming about playing for England, again. Cathy Hargreaves was filing her nails, again: while Trisha

Yates had her eyes closed and seemed to be asleep, again. All in all, a fairly normal lesson. Flippin' 'eck, thought Tucker, what's the point of all this? We might as well not be here. How does Sooty put up with it? Rabbiting on to a mob who don't give a monkey's.

'How do you reckon he puts up with it, Tommy?' he suddenly heard himself ask.

'Who?'

'Sooty.'

'What?'

'Put up with having to teach us, like.'

'Gets paid, doesn't he?'

'Yeah . . . but . . .'

But he wasn't allowed to finish as Mr Sutcliffe's voice broke in.

'Is that a private conversation, Jenkins? Or can we all join in?'

Tucker turned towards the front. He realized that all the scratching, dreaming, filing and sleeping had stopped and everyone was now paying attention, hoping something was going to happen to break the boredom.

'Sorry, sir?' The reply was automatic.

'Perhaps you'd like to tell us what you told Watson.'

'It were nothing, sir.'

'Come on, don't be bashful. I'm sure we'd all be fascinated to share your little secret.'

That's the trouble, thought Tucker. They're always as bored as us and so when they get the chance to liven things up, they won't let go.

'It was nothing,' Tucker repeated with a shrug.

'It must have been something more interesting than *She Stoops to Conquer*, Jenkins,' Sutcliffe pressed.

'That wouldn't take much,' someone muttered.

'Well?' Sutcliffe asked.

Tucker hesitated for a moment, but he'd known Sooty for a long time. He knew he was easy going, but he could tell by the tone of his voice he was beginning to wind himself up. Better give him something, thought Tucker, and then, what have I got to lose, I'll tell him.

'I was just asking Tommy how you put up with it all. That's all.'

Sutcliffe looked a bit puzzled. 'Put up with what?'

'This. Us. Rabbiting on about some crappy play when no one's taking a blind bit of notice.'

This brought a round of sniggers and giggles. All attention was then turned to Sutcliffe, who looked quite surprised.

'Because I'm paid to?' But the class just groaned. Obviously they wanted something more. 'Well, what do you expect me to say?' he asked, trying to retrieve the situation.

'Thought you were supposed to have a vocation,' Trisha chipped in.

'Yeah,' Cathy agreed. 'You're supposed to enjoy trying to teach us.'

'It's a bit difficult trying to teach people who don't want to be taught,' Sutcliffe countered.

'Not the way you lot teach it. It's so boring.'

'We don't want to be taught half the stuff you throw at us anyway,' Trisha added.

'Half?' Tommy snorted. 'All of it you mean.'

'Hang about, Tommy,' Tucker said. 'I like some of the stuff. We all have some things we like.'

'Yeah, like going home,' Trisha suggested.

'You know what I mean. I like Art and that. Benbo likes togger.'

'I like Music,' Cathy offered.

73

'Physics is O.K.,' someone else offered, but Sutcliffe brought the debate to a halt.

'All right, all right, we're not here to discuss the school curriculum.'

'What are we here for, then?' Tucker asked.

'To study *She Stoops to Conquer*,' Sutcliffe said, emphasizing each word by tapping the book.

'What's the point if we don't want to be taught?' Cathy said throwing his own words back at him.

A heavy silence settled over the room as the whole form waited for Sutcliffe's response. Tucker's honest answer had, quite by accident, unleashed a lot of pent-up frustration. Mr Sutcliffe recognized this fact through the transformation that had occurred before his eyes. Ironically, although Mr Sutcliffe should have condemned their behaviour and forced them to continue their appraisal of Goldsmith's classic play, he had never seen them all so united in a common desire for knowledge. Why *was* school so boring? It seemed like too good an opportunity to miss and what was more, he too, was bound by the same frustration.

'All right then!' he heard himself say. 'It's obvious we aren't going to get anywhere with this.' He dropped the book on to his desk. 'So let's take a look at the issue Jenkins has raised.'

There was an outbreak of grinning faces and a buzz of conversation went round the room. No one had expected this.

'Well, Jenkins,' Sutcliffe asked, 'would you care to expand on your thoughts for the benefit of us all?'

In one movement all heads turned towards Tucker.

'Well, Jenkins, Nothing more to say about me er . . . rabbiting on about some crappy play, I think was the phrase you used.' Tucker grinned. It sounded funny

74

coming out of Sutcliffe's mouth. Everyone else seemed to be enjoying the situation as well. Even if half of them were only enjoying his embarrassment.

'C'mon Jenkins. You always have so much to say for yourself. Don't let us all down now.'

Oh well, thought Tucker. He took a breath.

'Well, it's just . . . well . . . what's the point?'

'Of what?' Sutcliffe asked.

'Of making us read all this stuff. *The Ancient Mariner* and that. And old Billy Shakespeare. It's useless, isn't it?'

There were a good few nods and murmurs of agreement.

'Useless?' Sutcliffe enquired.

'Yeah.' Tucker shrugged. 'I mean, what's the point of it?'

'What's the point of any literature?'

'Dunno.' Tucker fingered his eye. A nervous gesture as he was finding it difficult expressing himself.

'You don't know. You say it's useless. But you don't know why it's useless?' Sutcliffe's voice rose higher and higher as an indication of disbelief. Everyone except Tucker was enjoying the performance.

'You know what I mean.'

'I'm afraid I don't. If *you* don't know what you mean, how am I supposed to know?'

This was getting out of hand. If I don't do something here he's going to make a right wally out of me, thought Tucker. Look at Doyley. Loving every minute of it he is. But his attention was pulled back to Mr Sutcliffe.

'So, Jenkins. Without a shred of explanation or qualification you are expecting us, as usual, to take your word that *She Stoops to Conquer*, an acknowledged classic for the past few hundred years I

75

might add, is . . . to quote you again . . . "useless". Is that a fair estimation of the situation?'

Tucker was now ready to slide under the desk. Old Sooty may be a pushover most of the time, but when his rag goes he's as hard as the best of them. He looked round for Tommy and Benny. Although both looked sympathetic, there wasn't much either could do. He'd dug his own grave and he must either let himself be buried in it, or he had to climb out himself. Well, I've gone this far, thought Tucker. Might as well go for a billy than a nanny. Here goes. 'It's just . . . well, what I mean . . .' The words were difficult in coming. '. . . the thing is. I don't know if the play's any good or not, do I?'

'Why?'

'Because er . . .' He decided to soften it with a grin, '. . . er . . . because I never listen, do I?'

The whole form exploded into laughter.

Sutcliffe looked astonished. 'And whose fault is that?'

'Yours.'

'Mine! I'd be interested to know how you figure that one out.'

'Well . . .' Another hesitation. Another grin. 'You make it sound so boring.'

'Do I, indeed?'

Tucker shrugged. 'You wanted to know.'

From the look on Mr Sutcliffe's face, he was beginning to regret the way the lesson was going. He picked up his copy of the book and waited a few moments to see if they quietened down. They didn't. Tucker was grinning again, and he was once more the unchallenged clown prince.

Suddenly everything stopped with a loud bang as Sutcliffe brought his book down hard against his desk.

'All right. That's quite enough.' He paused, both for effect and to let the last twitterings of conversation die a natural death. 'All right, Jenkins. We've all had a good laugh. Now, let's take a more serious look at the situation.'

The only person who looked pleased at this heavy-handed turn of events was Doyle, obviously hoping Tucker was now in trouble for being insolent. A similar thought was in Tucker's mind, and he held his breath waiting for Sooty's next statement. Fortunately, Sooty still wanted to mine this strange vein of interest he had accidentally unearthed.

'You think I'm boring do you, Jenkins?'

'Er . . . I never quite said that.'

'Oh? I thought you did.' He sounded a little peeved.

'Er . . . no, not really. I mean, you're O.K. As a bloke, like. Right lads?' He turned to Tommy and Benny who nodded their consent.

'Oh, well I'm glad to hear that at least. So . . . if I'm all right as a bloke, when am I boring?'

'When you start rabbiting on, you know.'

'About "crappy" plays? I get the picture. So, what you're saying is that it's not *me* that's boring. It might not even be the material I teach. But the way I teach it?'

'Er . . . yeah. Suppose I am.'

'I see.' Sutcliffe put his hands together and rested his forehead on his fingertips. Tucker looked across to Tommy and Benny again and shrugged, mouthing, 'He asked me, didn't he?' After a moment he looked up. 'Does anyone else think like Jenkins?'

'Huh, no one could think like him,' Trisha was quick to throw in, but Sutcliffe didn't see the joke.

'I am trying to be serious, Trisha.'

'Oh, sorry I spoke.' She sank back into her chair.

'Well? Do they?' Sutcliffe repeated.

One, two, three then four, six hands went up and slowly the whole form seemed to agree with Tucker. Sutcliffe clicked his tongue a few times, then stared at the floor. It had been quite a condemnation.

No one was quite sure what Sooty was thinking. Was he annoyed? Was he upset? He held his head down so long Trisha actually began to worry about him. In spite of their quick exchange and no matter how boring he was, he was still one of the best teachers in the school. At least he always made an effort to listen and help where he could. Not like the likes of Curtis, or Keating, or Bridget, or worst of all, Trisha's arch enemy, Miss Clark. Trisha was beginning to feel concerned. She'd never seen Sooty like this before. No one had. Was he really upset? He looked it. After all he had just been accused of not doing his job properly. Trisha turned and glared at Tucker accusingly and he could feel the mood of support shifting from his clownish antics towards Sooty. Trisha jerked her head for Tucker to say something. All eyes turned towards him once again.

How did I get myself into this, he thought. Flippin' Sooty's supposed to be in command here. Not me. He looked back at Trisha. How the hell should I know what to say? She raised her eyes, and turned back to Sutcliffe. Someone had to say something. So she closed her eyes to gather her thoughts and then leaped in.

'Er . . . you all right, sir?' she ventured. To her surprise Sutcliffe looked up, with a small smile on his lips.

'Oh . . . yes, sorry, I was just thinking.'

'Bloomin' 'eck! We thought you were going to burst into tears for a moment.'

78

'What? Oh no.' His smile broadened. 'I just found it ironic. Here we are. All struggling through Goldsmith and *all* bored out of our minds.'

'You mean *you* are too?' Cathy asked, a bit incredulous.

Sutcliffe nodded. 'It's not easy out here, you know.'

'Must be easier than being back here,' Tucker offered.

'You should try it, sometime.'

'Don't want to show you up,' quipped Tucker, glad to be exchanging verbal thrusts once again.

Trisha sat up in her chair. 'Yeah . . . why don't you, mighty mouth?'

'Yeah,' Doyle picked it up. 'Think you could do better, Jenkins?'

A slow murmur of similar suggestion began to spread around the class. Eventually Sutcliffe had to bang the book on the desk again. 'O.K. O.K.' Everyone quietened down. 'Well, Jenkins? Do you think you could do a better job?'

'Not with this stuff, I couldn't.'

'But I thought we said it wasn't the material taught, but the *way* it was taught. How ideas are put across. I'm sure a man with your obvious creative imagination could make anything sound interesting.'

Tucker could see himself being forced into a corner. The sympathies of the class were definitely behind Sooty this morning. He had to start talking, and fast.

'C'mon, sir. You know that's not fair.'

'Oh, why not?'

'Well . . . I don't know anything about this stuff, do I?'

'Perhaps you should have paid more attention, then.'

This is crazy, Tucker thought. How do I manage to get myself into these situations? He flippin' well asked me what I thought, so why am I suddenly getting the aggro? 'That's down to you to make it interesting enough to make me want to pay attention, isn't it?'

That was the real nub of it, as far as Tucker was concerned. It was Sooty's job. I mean, he carried on thinking, this mob can even make games boring. We often spend all break and all lunchtime playing footey, but as soon as we have to do it in games we start to skive off. Crazy. But Sutcliffe was coming back at him.

'All right, Jenkins. Then suppose you come out here. Pick your own subject. Your own hobby, perhaps. Something you personally like or enjoy. Then tell us why you like it. And try and make us appreciate it?' Tucker's heart sank. He should have expected this when Sooty jumped on to the 'do you think you could do better' routine. He looked around the room. All eyes were turned towards him. Tommy and Benny showed some sympathy, not much, but some. Trisha, Cathy and Doyle, especially Doyle, were obviously waiting for him to drop one. Everyone else was just enjoying the situation. Well, it was better than Sooty's play, wasn't it?

Got to be careful here, he thought. If I go out there now I'll make a right idiot of myself. And if I back down he'd never let me forget it, would he? Flippin' 'eck. How do I manage it?

'Well, Jenkins? Not an attractive proposition is it?'

It certainly isn't, agreed Tucker. But he was determined, as usual, not to let anyone, never mind Sooty, get the better of him. He tried an alternative route. 'Er . . . I'm not prepared, am I? I mean, you get time to make notes and that, don't you? So it's not fair just asking me to jump straight in, like.' All heads turned back towards Sutcliffe. That seemed like a reasonable point.

'All right,' Sutcliffe agreed. 'You can prepare something for the next period. Anything you like.' At least that was something, Tucker thought. But Trisha spoke up.

'I don't think it should be "anything he likes", sir. I mean it should be what he likes, but not his choice, if you see what I mean. To be a proper er . . . test, it should be something he likes, but none of us do. If you see what I mean.'

'Like smacking people in the mouth, who can't mind their own business,' Tucker said, only half-joking.

'Good point, Trisha.' Sutcliffe grinned. 'Any suggestions?' He threw it out to the class. For a moment no one came up with anything, until Doyle said, 'What about the way he likes to shout his mouth off. None of us like that.'

'You're the expert on that, Doyley.' Tucker was quick to respond.

'He can talk about anything, as far as I'm concerned,' said Cathy. 'I can't stand anything he does.'

This brought a round of chuckles. Then Mary Johnson put up her hand. 'What about motorbikes? He's interested in them. And I'm not.'

Most of the girls agreed. The boys didn't seem to care and as the changeover bell went, Sutcliffe was glad to find something. 'O.K. Motorbikes it is. Next time, Jenkins.' He grinned as he moved to the door. 'I'm looking forward to it already.'

'Landed yourself in it there, Tucker,' Benny said as they made their way towards Woodwork.

'What else is new?' Tommy chuckled.

'Don't make it too exciting, will you?' Trisha said sarcastically as she passed him in the corridor. 'I use that lesson to catch up on my beauty sleep.'

'Looks like you've still got a long way to go then.' Tucker couldn't help grinning. One thing about Pongo. She was always there with some comment or other. If she wasn't who she was, and if they hadn't fought like cat and dog all these years, and if she wasn't more often than not having a go at him, he thought, he might just fancy . . . but he forced the thought out of his mind. Him and Pongo? Never! His mind went back to his talk on motorbikes, and his body went off to Woodwork.

Throughout the following week Tucker read and re-read through the motorbike magazines he had stacked in one corner of his room. Every time his mother came into his room and saw him going through them she said the same old thing: 'Sorting them out to throw away, at long last?' If she had her way, Tucker thought, I'd only have the bed and wardrobe in here. And I bet she'd really like me not to sleep in the bed, so she wouldn't have to make it.

The night before he was due to give his talk, Tucker finally admitted he had a problem. He couldn't figure out why he *did* like motorbikes. He just did. You do, don't you, he told himself. You either like something or you don't. It gets to you. I know that, dimbo, but why? That's what you've got to tell 'em. Not just that, but you've got to make them understand it as well. You've got to make it get to them, too. Bloomin' Sooty, he groaned as he lay on his back and fired a paper pellet at the Lancaster bomber diving towards him out of the sun – well, the bedroom light. Missed. He tore out a page of his rough work book and started to make a new supply of pellets. As he did, his mind suddenly jumped back to his very first day at Grange Hill. He had been caught firing paper pellets by that games master. He grinned as he remembered it. A cracking shot at the back of Pongo Yates's head. Zap. Right on the bonce. He rolled off the bed and fired at the Lancaster. A hit. Port wing. The bomber flipped up and then dropped and was left spinning on the fishing cord that suspended it from the ceiling.

He lay on the floor and let his mind drift back to that first day. Of course he hadn't known it was Pongo Yates at the time, but that pellet probably started off their enmity. Well, it wasn't just that. He remembered how he'd been left off the register and how he'd had to go with that stupid Mrs Dunne. Right wally she was, thought Tucker. Kept forgetting my name. Bet she wouldn't now, he grinned, as he had a shot at the Phantom, banking away towards the windows. A miss.

He then remembered that when she had found out where he was supposed to be and taken him along to his class, he found himself sitting in front of Pongo. As soon as she saw him she belted him over the head with her ruler. He chuckled. He'd never known a girl to stick up for herself like she did. She's crackerbarrel really, he told himself. If half the blokes I know had half the bottle she's got, they'd be doing O.K., he thought as he once again blasted the crippled Lancaster. All I hope now, he continued, is that I've got the bottle to see it through tomorrow.

It took him a long time to get to sleep that night, as he still didn't have a clue what he was going to say.

How do you get across to someone why you like something, if you don't know yourself, let alone make them like it? He was already beginning to see why Sooty got so cheesed off.

Next morning he was up early and decided to walk down to the Bike Shop. The magazines had scored a zilch in the inspiration department and he was hoping that a sight of the real thing might spark off some understanding.

He stood and stared in at the rows of bikes for about thirty minutes. His eyes swept across the Hondas, Suzukis, Yamahas and settled on his personal favourite, the Kawasaki Green. 1300cc, water cooled, six cylinder, prop-driven. 0–60 in 4·5 seconds. Ace! Yeah, but why, he kept asking himself. Looks good, doesn't it? Looks powerful. It *is* powerful, dimbo. Is that it? Because it goes like a rocket? Why should that be such a big deal? It is to me. Yeah, but why?

He shrugged and turned away. He found motorbikes fascinating. The idea of going so fast, so quickly. But he knew other people didn't. Benny didn't. Neither did Alan. They both liked looking at them, but neither of them was as keen as him. As he was about to cross the road, he took one look back. How could you explain it to other people? The likes of Pongo just wouldn't have a clue about what you were on about, he thought as he turned the corner into the street outside the school. A motorbike's a motorbike as far as they're concerned. They wouldn't appreciate the amount of design and engineering work that it takes to put something like the Kawasaki together. Then his light bulb lit up. I wonder if . . . he thought. Yeah, that's probably . . . You don't think about that, do you? But some bloke's had to sit down and work out how to squeeze it all in, hasn't he?

And the shape of each bit and that, so it works properly. And then how it looks. Inside the engine you can do what you like, really, so long as it works properly. Its appearance doesn't really matter. You can leave metal looking like metal. But on the outside it's different, isn't it? People like to see a bit of flash. The old chrome and metallic paint. Corker! That's it, isn't it? Appreciating what's gone into it! Yeah.

He'd reached the gate by this time and just as he was about to enter, a small trail bike pulled up and a third year got off the back. Tucker didn't know who it was but it looked like an older brother on the front. Tucker sauntered over to the bike as the third year went through the gate.

'This yours?' Tucker asked.

'No, it's his. I'm just minding it for him,' the rider said sarcastically.

Tucker grinned. Fair comment, he thought. Stupid question. He then thought he'd try out his new theory.

'Why'd you pick this bike?' The rider just shrugged.

'Did you think about all the design effort and that that's gone into it?' Tucker asked.

'You what?' the rider was incredulous. 'It was bleedin' cheap and it goes like a rocket.' He kicked it over, did a wheelie and sped off.

Some rocket, Tucker thought. Compared to the Kawasaki it was more like an angry bee!

As Tucker turned into the form room for registration, he was aware that there was an air of expectancy. Tommy and Benny were already waiting for him.

'Today's the day then, Tucker,' said Tommy.

'Got your speech ready?' asked Benny.

'I'm not making any speech,' Tucker said. 'I'll just

tell you bikes are ace and you'll trust me, won't you?'

'Some chance.'

'Just like that?' Tommy asked.

'Don't you believe everything I say, Tommy?'

'Oh yeah. I was forgetting about that,' Tommy said sarcastically.

During registration Tucker thought back to the guy on the trail bike. 'Because it was cheap.' That was the first thing he'd said. But he'd also said it went like a rocket. Well, thought Tucker, suppose it depends on how fast you like your rockets. Still, it was still a sign that the guy was interested in the power behind the bike. So he must have some interest in the design and engineering of it, thought Tucker. Even if he doesn't know it himself. And if he did he'd probably get more out of it. Be able to appreciate it more like. Tucker grinned again, he was beginning to sound like Sooty. He couldn't be right after all could he?

By the time registration ended Tucker had realized that at least one aspect of his dispute with Sooty was resolved. You *could* get more out of something if you knew exactly what went into it. But as he made his way towards English he knew there was still the main problem. How to convince someone who didn't want to know? No one had been able to do it to him since he'd been at Grange Hill. Worse still, how do you attempt it with a mob who were probably going to do their best to make you look like an idiot?

The reception he got was exactly what he had expected. There were a few 'wheeays' as he walked in and sat down to wait for Sutcliffe and then it really began.

'Ready to make a complete fool of yourself then, Jenkins?' Doyle shouted from the back and banged his desk lid up and down to emphasize the point.

'Thought he'd have got well tired of that by now, wouldn't you?' added Trisha. Fortunately, it didn't go on too long as Sooty was on time for once.

'Right, Peter. You ready to turn us all on to the exciting world of motorbikes?'

Tucker hesitated for a moment, feeling all the eyes focusing on him. Then he forced his body to let go of its grip on the chair and got to his feet. As he walked down the aisle he could see that even Sooty had a smirk on his face.

He reached the front and turned to face the class. Doyle was half-turned in his chair leaning against the wall, grinning from ear to ear in expectation. Trisha was slumped down in her seat and Cathy had already taken out her nail file.

'Right, Peter,' Sutcliffe said. 'Let's hear it.'

Tucker stood for a moment slowly looking round. He looked as though he was weighing up everybody, but he was trying to find some way of moistening his mouth so that the piece of sandpaper that had once been his tongue could move about more freely. After a moment or two, Doyle couldn't resist commenting, 'Dead interesting this is, isn't it? What you talking about now? Silencers?'

'Quiet, Doyle, or outside,' Sutcliffe snapped. 'C'mon, Peter.'

Flippin' 'eck, thought Tucker. How'd I get out of this? How'd I get into it? Too late now anyway. Just start, go on.

'Er . . . I was going to er . . .' His voice suddenly started up. 'Start off by saying how great motorbikes and that were, but er . . . I think that er . . . depends on whether you like 'em or not.'

'Thought you were supposed to make us like them?' Trisha teased.

Tucker decided to ignore her, so continued 'Er . . . but I thought I'd tell you why I like 'em. And er . . . why you should like them.' At least, and at last, he'd started.

He then went on to talk about the different sizes and shapes, and the different engines and styles. But all the time he went on about how much design and effort went into them. How he appreciated it, as a piece of engineering. How the thought of going at 120 mph on what was only a piece of metal, really, excited him. And so on and so on. After about fifteen of the worst minutes of his life he looked round to see the result. He had been trying to avoid any eye contact up to this point and had been looking at the ceiling, at the door, out of the window. Anywhere except at his audience.

When he did finally look, the sight that greeted him made him smile. Doyle was scratching something else into the desk; Benny was looking out of the window, probably playing in some cup final; Cathy was filing her nails and Trisha looked like she was asleep! However, as soon as he stopped speaking, Trisha spoke. She didn't open her eyes but just said in a fairly loud voice, 'Thank God he's finished. C'mon, sir, even Shakespeare's better than this boring load of rubbish.'

He turned and looked at Sutcliffe who was sitting on the front desk leaning against the wall, a huge grin on his face as he had watched Tucker's eyes slowly going round the room. Tucker sighed then broke into a huge grin.

'O.K. . . . . you win!' he said to Sutcliffe.

'It's not as easy as it looks,' Sutcliffe replied as he swung himself upright and crossed to his own desk. 'I hope you've learned something, though, Peter.'

'To keep his trap shut, I hope,' said Trisha.

Tucker nodded at Sutcliffe. 'I know what you mean about appreciating something more if you learn more about it now.'

'Huh, the more we learn about *you*, the less we appreciate!' Trisha snorted.

Tucker bit his lip as he walked back to his seat. She's always there, isn't she, he thought. Once she gets her teeth into you there's no shaking her off. I'll never live this down. Never.

'I hope your newfound appreciation will mean you'll pay more attention from now on, Peter?'

'I may have learned to appreciate you, sir. But . . .' He grinned. 'That doesn't make the lesson any less boring!'

Sutcliffe just grinned. The exercise had been worthwhile from Tucker's point of view. If only he could think of some way of reaching the other thirty-three!

Maybe Tomorrow

This time, thought Tucker. This time I'll do it. Straight across. Up the path and knock on the door. I was er . . . just passing and thought I'd . . . Nah, too corny. Come straight out with it, that's best. Yeah. Right then. Straight across. Up the path. Ding-dong. Fancy coming out with us tonight? Yeah. That's it. Straight in, no messing. O.K. Here goes. He stepped out from behind the wall he had been leaning against and started across the road. This time he reached the middle before his stomach started jumping up and down inside his chest and the doubts crept back into his head. What if her mum answers the door? Or her dad. Or her sister. Yeah what about her? I'm not standing there while she goes off and tells her. Laughing her socks off. Specially if she says no. Be all round the school tomorrow. Flippin' 'eck! By this time he had spun round and was now safely behind the wall, out of sight from the house. He leaned back, resting his head against the wall. This is crazy. You'll never know if you don't get over there and ask her, dimbo. He had been telling himself the same thing over and over again for the past hour. It was getting a bit ridiculous. Good job I did come on me own. I could imagine what Tommy'd make of this. He took several quick but deep breaths in an attempt to calm down.

He looked down at his hands to see they were shaking. Even going up against the Brookies I don't feel like this. C'mon Jenkins. Get your act together. A couple more breaths. Right then, this time. Across. Ding-dong. You comin' out or not? Right. With a determined push he propelled himself off the wall, rounded the corner and was just about to start across the road when the front door opened and she came out with her mother.

That's all I need. Tucker groaned as he did another fast retreat. I can't ask her out in front of her mother. Better leave it until tomorrow. Yeah. No rush, is there? Might as well get it right. He ambled off down the road. Giving up, for the third successive night. I'll definitely do it tomorrow. I will. Tomorrow.

By the time he was crossing the square towards the stairs that led to their maisonette, Tucker had convinced himself things had worked out for the best. Funny how that had happened on the previous two nights as well. Still, tomorrow would be the day when he would definitely and finally ask Trisha Yates out. He'd made up his mind. No bones about it this time. It was all set. Just as it had been the other two nights. He went straight up to the pigsty, as his mother still called his bedroom, pushed a pile of clothes off the bed, hung them on the floor and dropped on to the bed.

'God, I fancy her though,' he said to himself as he folded his hands behind his head. He couldn't think why. She's not really my type, is she? Bit too skinny. Like 'em with a bit more meat on 'em. Like Pamela Cartwright. Still, that one was over now. But why did he fancy Pongo Yates? That's what he couldn't figure out.

He tried to remember when he got the first twinge, but it was difficult. All he could think about was the times he'd had to struggle with her. Right on their first day at Grange Hill they'd had a set-to. Got her on the back of the head with a paper pellet. He laughed at the memory. Good shot it was too. And then that PE bloke knuckled me. What was his name now? Fraser? No. Foster. Yeah. Frosty Foster. Rabbiting on about putting people's eyes out. Stupid berk.

'Peter!' his mum suddenly called from downstairs.

'Yeah?'

'You in for your tea?'

'Yeah.'

'Then come down here and help lay the table.'

He pulled a face but didn't answer, hoping she would go away. Why couldn't she do it? But she wouldn't.

'Peter!'

'All right. I'll be down in a minute.' He knew it was pointless to try and get out of it. His mind went back to those very first days at Grange Hill all that time ago, and he found himself chuckling again. She pushed me over too. When me and Benny were messing about with that soppy Judy Preston. First girl who'd ever had the guts to stick up for herself. Right trouble we had. Wouldn't mind wrestling with her now, though.

'Peter!' His mum's voice again, sounding like the third and final public warning. He looked at his watch, then raised his eyes as he realized he had wasted two hours hovering outside Yatesey's. I'll definitely do it tomorrow, he thought as he swung his legs off the bed.

After tea he wandered down towards Tommy's and was only half surprised to find himself taking a two

mile short cut that took him past Trisha's house. He
didn't even hover on the corner this time. He'd had
enough of that for today. Tomorrow was the time. He
just decided to pass. Just in case. You never knew. She
might have come out. But what'd I say if she did, he
suddenly thought as he came level with her front door,
trying to look out the side of his eye for signs of life
without appearing too obvious. She'd never take me
seriously, would she? She'd think I was winding her up
if I just bumped into her. That's going to be a big
problem, that is. So that's why it'd best be done by
calling, right. Then she'd have to believe it. If I'd made
a special journey, like.

He was now level with the path. Shall I do it now? All
I need do is turn and I'm halfway there. Shall I? But he
was now three steps past. I can't go back now. She
might see me go past and then turn back. She'd know I
was nervous then. Well, you are. I know, but she
doesn't have to know, does she? She might not have
seen me, though. Probably hasn't. Shall I go back? He
slowed down, but only for a moment. Nah. Do it
tomorrow! He crossed the road and headed off for
Tommy's, a wry smile on his face. Doing a Benny here,
I am. He made his famous chicken noise, almost
without realizing it, which brought a surprised look
from an old boy painting his garden gnomes.

After collecting Tommy, Benny was next on the list
and then Alan. It was one of the nights that Susi
washed her hair and so Alan was allowed out to play.

'Under there, you are!' Tommy said, holding his
thumb upside down.

'You'll be under mine, in a minute,' Alan replied. He
always got a bit niggly when anyone went on about the
way Susi bossed him about, although he knew it was

true. Both perfectly valid reasons for Tommy to keep rubbing it in.

'When you get engaged where's she going to put the ring? On her finger, or through your nose?'

Alan made a grab for him, but Tommy was expecting it and dived behind Benny, who took the full weight of Alan's massive frame.

'Jack it in, will you?' Benny moaned, as he pushed them away. Tommy decided to walk in the gutter, and keep some distance between him and Alan for a few minutes.

'Where we going, Tucker?'

'Where'd we usually go?' Tucker replied.

Benny shrugged. 'Nowhere special.'

'Then we're going there again, aren't we?'

They continued their seemingly aimless wandering for a few more minutes before someone wanted some direction in their life.

'Let's go down the precinct and stick putty in the locks again?' Tommy suggested.

'Don't you ever grow up?' Alan enquired.

'Not if I can help it, grandad.'

Alan just pulled a face. 'I'm starving.'

'What else is new?' said Benny.

'Let's go down the Big M, then.'

No one replied.

'Tucker?'

'I'm skint.'

'As I said,' continued Benny, 'what else is new?'

'I've got some bread,' Tommy offered. 'Enough for a couple of shakes.'

'I've got my own,' said Alan.

'I'm not hungry,' said Benny. He never was. He never had any money either.

'I'll get you a shake,' Tommy offered. 'We on then?'

They all nodded. Alan turned to Tommy, 'Except you!' Tommy looked puzzled. Alan gave an exaggerated sniff, 'You're always a bit off!'

Benny and Tucker groaned.

'You want to be careful there, Al,' Tommy replied quickly. 'That was almost a joke!'

As they all set off for Ronald McDonalds, Benny turned to Tucker.

'Here, doesn't Pongo Yates live around here somewhere?'

'Does she?' Tucker replied, sounding innocent. 'Thought she lived over on Oakfield.'

'Nah. Round here somewhere.'

'Oh.'

No one thought much of it, just as none of the others noticed Tucker looking back over his shoulder as they turned a corner and passed a wall that seemed more than a little familiar.

'Do you have to?' Tommy complained at the disgusting noise Alan was making trying to suck the bottom of his shake up through the straw.

'Best bit the last bit.'

'Then you should drink that first, shouldn't you?'

'How am I supposed to do that, soft head?'

'You could try holding it upside down.'

Alan just pulled a face, and slurped his shake once again.

'What's happening now?' Benny wanted to know.

'We're about to make ourselves sick listening to Hogs-Head, over there,' Tommy muttered, which only served to bring another louder slurp and then a huge burp from Alan.

'You can't take him anywhere, can you?'

'C'mon, Tucker. You've hardly spoken all night. What's up?' enquired Benny.

'Nothing,' replied Tucker.

'You O.K.?' asked Tommy.

'Yeah.'

'Well, what are we going to do?' Benny continued.

No one had any suggestions. All looked to Tucker, who just shrugged.

'Let's go down the precinct on the blimp then,' Tommy offered. No one took it up. 'Tucker?'

'Nah . . . not tonight, Tom.'

'Great night out with the lads this has turned out to be. Couple of miles on the road and a chocolate shake. Terrific.'

'What else do we normally do?' asked Benny, echoing Tucker earlier.

'Have a laugh while we're about it!' He turned to Tucker who didn't seem to be listening to them but staring into the bottom of his shake cup. His mind had gone back to the vexing problem of why he found himself fancying Trisha Yates. Imagine it! Him and Pongo!

Everyone knew that they hated each other. Like cat and dog it was. Always had been. Always trying to put the other down. Until just recently. At least as far as Tucker was concerned. He had decided it was probably at the Christmas Dance that he had first got the twinge. He couldn't think why, but he did remember giving her more than the perfunctory glance. At one stage he'd even thought about looking for some mistletoe, but he'd planned that as another wind-up. At least that's what he thought at the time. Now he wasn't so sure.

His thoughts were interrupted by a sharp bang on

the arm and he looked up to see Tommy speaking to him.

'Why are you the life and soul of the party tonight, anyway?'

'What . . . sorry lads,' Tucker offered lamely. 'Just got something on me mind, that's all.'

'Anything we can help with?' Alan asked.

'No.' Tucker smiled.

'Not homework, I hope?' asked Tommy.

Tucker grinned. 'No way.'

'Thank God for that. I'd have really been worried then.'

Tucker grinned. If he knew the real reason he'd definitely have been worried. And I'd never get a moment's peace again!

When they left the Big M they still hadn't solved the problem of how to spend the evening.

'Let's go down the precinct,' Tommy urged.

'You got shares in that place, or something?' Alan asked.

'At least we can always find something to do down there.'

'Like what?'

'I don't know, do I? We're not there yet.'

'We could always look in the wallpaper shop window,' Benny said in derision.

'Yeah. And there's a great building society up-stairs.'

'Cor – is there!' Benny mocked.

'And a dress shop. Tommy'll like that.'

'All right, smart arse. You got any better ideas?' Tommy asked.

'Yeah. Going home and watching the match,' Benny suggested.

'It's not on till half-ten. What about you, Tucker?'

'Not fussy.' He shrugged.

'We can see that by the state of your jeans,' Tommy was quick to come in with. Then he found himself toppled over the small wall surrounding the flower beds outside the library.

'Pack it in, Tucker.'

'Sorry, Tom. Didn't see you on the end of me boot, then.'

'C'mon. What we going to do?' asked Alan.

'Dunno.' Tucker shrugged again.

'Well, I still say we go to the precinct.' Tommy tried again as he climbed out of the flower bed. The others all raised their eyes. 'It's somewhere to go, isn't it? And at least we can look in the shops. Proper shops,' he emphasized at Alan and Benny. 'Like the stereo centre and Multi-sounds and that. C'mon, it's better than hanging about here and being picked on by the Old Bill, isn't it?'

The others finally accepted the logic.

'Yeah,' said Tucker. 'Why get picked up here, when we can do it in more style in the precinct?' They started to walk away but Tucker stopped.

'Watch it, Tommy!'

'Why?' Tommy turned around in surprise, thinking something was coming at him from behind. Which is exactly what Tucker wanted.

'In case you fall over the wall again!' he said as he pushed him backwards into the flower bed.

'I'll do . . .' Tommy spluttered, but his words were lost as he scrambled out and took off after Tucker.

'I'd get one of those,' Benny pointed to one of the newer personal hi-fi systems.

'Nah,' Tucker said. 'That's only FM. That's what

I'd go for.' He pointed to the very latest stereo-cassette/radio.

'Come in handy in old Sooty's lesson that would. You could stuff it in your coat and record what he was saying, while you listened to the radio. Crackerbarrel, that is.'

'Bit pricey, though,' Alan muttered.

'Soon pay that off on H.P. Once you're on the dole.'

'I'm staying on, I am,' Tommy announced.

'Leave it out, Tommy,' Tucker said. 'They wouldn't put up with you for another two years.'

'I'm not leaving next year. Not if the dole queues are still the same. Might as well stay on and see how it goes.' They all gave nods of agreement. What was the point of leaving school if you couldn't get a job? But then thoughts were brought back to a more immediate problem.

'Watch it!' Benny suddenly hissed.

They all turned to see a group of about seven blokes walking down the precinct towards them. Instinctively they went on to Red Alert. Just in case. Tucker stepped away from the stereo centre window so he could get a better view. Benny started watching their backs and looking for an escape route. Tommy let his wristwatch down his wrist and over his knuckles while Alan zipped up his jacket. Just in case.

'Know 'em?' Tucker asked.

Tommy shook his head. Neither of the other two recognized anyone, as the approaching gang had now obviously seen them. They fanned out. One of them started watching their backs and they all took their hands out of their pockets, zipped up their jackets and generally got themselves ready. Just in case.

This was the only disadvantage, at least in Tommy's

102

book, of hanging about the precinct. You were likely to get stepped on.

As the gap closed between the two groups the approaching gang moved across the precinct.

It looked as though they were moving into a line-up position. No one spoke. No one took their eyes off them. As they approached, Tucker and Co slowly turned so they were always face-on to the approaching group. Tucker clenched and unclenched his fists. He looked down at his hands. Steady as a rock. None of the shaking he had experienced outside Trisha Yates's. But this was different. He knew the odds here. He knew with a certainty bred of his fifteen years' survival training. He knew what signs to look for. What would happen, and, what was more, he knew exactly what to do. He knew he could handle it, if necessary.

Tucker risked a quick sideways glance. Tommy was looking a bit pale, licking his lips. Alan was standing, impassive, as though he was waiting to be served at the Tuck Shop. Benny was getting a bit fidgety, eyes bouncing all over the place. All perfectly normal. The troops were ready, if necessary.

The approaching group were by now level with them. If they were going to try and stamp on them, this would be it. The guy who appeared to be their leader slowed down, then stopped. Tucker heard Tommy swallow. This looked like it. The opposing team fanned out either side of their leader as he stood and took a long hard look at Tucker, then Alan, Tommy and Benny. His eyes came back to Alan, always a formidable sight and Tucker was sure his very size had saved them on several occasions. For almost two minutes they stood facing each other. It had to happen now. Outnumbered seven to four, Tucker almost felt an urge to take the three steps that separated them and strike first so they stood a chance of making a getaway. However, before he could make the decision the others moved, not forward but away to the right. They weren't looking for aggro after all, but making the point that they were ready and prepared. Just in case.

Tucker and Tommy let out a sigh of relief. Alan started to unzip his jacket and Benny fell against the shop window. He unclenched his hands and wiped the sweat away on his jeans. The danger had passed and the other team were now moving quickly away, but with two of their guys keeping a watch on Tucker and the others. Just in case.

'What did you say, Tom? There's always something to do, or *someone* to do, down here?' Benny asked.

'More like always someone to do you!' Tucker said as he watched the other team turn a corner and disappear from sight.

'Well, I've had enough laughs down here for one night,' Alan said, forcing the words out through a huge yawn.

'Yeah,' Benny agreed. 'I'm going home to watch the match. You coming, Tucker?'

Tucker nodded and started the exodus.

'Might as well have been out with me granny tonight,' Tommy moaned as he followed the others.

'She'd have been terrific against that lot,' Tucker said.

'She'd have dropped them all, my granny. One swipe of her walking stick . . . zap!'

The walk home was as uneventful and as boring as it usually was, with Benny and Alan peeling off at their homes. Tommy accompanied Tucker as far as the steps leading up to Tucker's landing. He had expected to be invited in for a cup of tea and toast, but he was out of luck.

'See you tomorrow then, Tom!' Tucker announced as he trudged wearily up the stairs.

'You going in, then?' Tommy complained.

'Yeah. That's why I'm going up these steps. Because I'm knackered and they lead to our house. See ya.' Then he was gone. Tommy had no alternative but to turn and head for home, kicking a coke can across the square as he went. Some night out.

If he had hung about a few minutes longer he would have seen Tucker reappear at the top of the steps, look to see if he had gone and then practically leap down the steps and dash across the square. So much for being knackered.

An hour later he really was knackered. He was back on his wall, watching Trisha's house and hoping she had been out somewhere and he could catch her on her way in. Unfortunately the only thing he looked like catching was a cold as it started to rain. Another ten minutes, he decided, then I'm off home. He didn't need the ten minutes because the front door opened and Trisha came out. For a moment he stopped breathing, but soon started again as she put a few milk bottles on the step and closed the door. Even from where he was standing Tucker could hear a bolt going on the door and when all the downstairs lights went out he realized that was it for tonight. He turned and headed back home. Definitely tomorrow then.

Tomorrow duly arrived, as it always seems to, but Trisha didn't. She didn't turn in for morning registration, nor that afternoon. The following day Cathy

Hargreaves brought in the news that she had flu and would be away for about a week. Terrific, thought Tucker, that's all I needed. Still, it saved him all those wasted hours propping up that wall. He could turn his mind to other things until she reappeared at school; or so he thought.

'Come on, Jenkins!' 'Pay attention, Jenkins!' 'Dreaming again, Jenkins?' That's all he seemed to hear for the next week. Not that it was that unusual. He very rarely paid attention these days, which meant that he was getting caught. Usually he always kept one tiny bit of his brain on the lookout for someone trying to score off him with the old 'What did I just say, Jenkins?' but he kept finding teachers coming at him sideways. Of course his mind was always on Trisha, or why he had suddenly started to fancy her. Then when Miss Mooney caught him out in Assembly one day, he decided that was it. The last straw.

Enough's enough, Tucker me old lad, he thought as he trudged off to detention for the zillionth time. He flopped down in what was now his usual desk, took out a pen and notebook, started doodling and going over the situation once again. She's having a bad influence on you, mate. You either go through with it or forget her. Right? Right. But he'd just spent a week trying to forget. You'll have to get it together and ask her then, won't you? Even if she does blow you out, you'll have sorted it one way or the other. Right? Right. I mean, can't have Mooney getting the drop on you, can you? As soon as you see her, you ask her, regardless of where it is, and who she's with. Right? Right. No matter who it is. And who they might tell. No matter what it does to your image. You get this nonsense over. You do it. Right? Er . . . I'll let you know.

When Trisha eventually returned to school, the first time Tucker saw her answered the one question that had been going round and round his head. Why did he fancy her? I mean, he used to tell himself, she's not that fantastic to look at. She's not a robber's dog, like, but she's not a classic, is she? She's not mastermind, is she, although on second thoughts he decided that would have been a turn off anyway. She doesn't even like motorbikes. Must be something, though.

His mind was still working on this as he turned into the main teaching block. He wasn't looking where he was going and collided with someone coming through the door . . . Trisha.

'Bloomin' 'eck, you blind or something?'

'Er . . . sorry . . . I was thinking about . . .' he tried to stammer an apology, but she cut him off.

'I thought you looked in agony!' she said, and with that she was gone.

Tucker grinned, that was it. Over the years she was probably the only one in the entire school who had repeatedly got the better of him. Not in any big way, but in the continual clashes and verbal exchanges. She always gave as good as she got. As he leaned against the door and watched her cross the yard, he realized that when he had often called her a pain in the bum, he actually respected her. He liked the way she would stick up for herself and her mates. Like the time she helped organize the campaign against school uniform, for all the good it did. Still, he thought, took a lot of guts that.

'What you grinning at?' a voice suddenly asked from behind.

Tucker turned to see it was Tommy. 'Oh . . nothing.'

'What's up with you lately?' Tommy sounded quite concerned.

'What do you mean?'

'You're never here these days. Always in the clouds somewhere.'

'I'm in love, aren't I?' Tucker announced, knowing it was the sort of answer Tommy would never believe.

'Oh yeah. Who with?'

'Bridget,' Tucker replied and walked on.

Right then. Now you know why you fancy her, what you going to do about it, Jenkins? He started on the self-analysis bit again. Ask her, I suppose. That's what I decided. Right, but when? Soon as I can. Could have done it then really. Should have done. Why didn't you? She took me by surprise, didn't she? O.K. That was then. But you take her by surprise later. When? At break. Right? Right.

Of course, break came and went and Trisha still wasn't taken by surprise. She nearly was at lunchtime but just as he was about to walk over to her, Cathy, Mary, Susi and Pamela joined her. No matter what he'd said to himself about doing it whoever she was with, that was stretching it just a bit too far.

Two days later he was back on his wall and counting up all the times he could have done it at school. She had been last out of Maths yesterday. She was first in English today. She had been alone at lunchtime today and had walked home alone yesterday. Plenty of opportunities, he thought, you just didn't have the bottle. All right, I know that now. It's no point thinking about asking her in school. Too many people. Too many people who know what I've always said about her. So it has to be here. Now. Tonight. Yes. It's got to be tonight or she'll start noticing, won't she? Bound to. Every time she's alone I'm there aren't I? Yeah, but she won't know what you're up to, will she? Blimey, probably last thing she'd think of. Last thing anyone would think of. Are you ready then? Yeah. Well go on then. Get it over with. He wanted to, but then he didn't. What if she says no? Then it's over and done, isn't it? Go on.

Finally, he took a huge breath, closed his eyes, counted to ten, pulled himself off the wall and set off across the road.

His stomach was doing somersaults. His mouth was drying up, but he could feel the sweat on his hands. If she says no, you're going to look a right clown. I'm doing that already, aren't I? Let's get it over, one way or the other. He was halfway across the road. Another wave of panic swept over him. What if she says yes? What then? You go out with her, bubble brain. Yeah, but where? Sort that out later. Just get up to that door and find out first. He was now right in front of the house and discovered his legs wouldn't go any further than the gate. C'mon, c'mon. Do it. It's too late to turn back, someone's bound to have seen you, by now. Get it over.

With a fair amount of effort he forced his left leg to move and then his right one to follow it. He reached the door and pressed the bell. That's it. Point of no return. He waited for a moment, his stomach now looping the loop, but no answer. There's no one in, he thought and the desire to go almost overwhelmed him. Beat a retreat while he still could. They might be out in the back. You're here now. Go through with it. He pressed the bell again. No answer. Right, that's it. She had her chance. Hang about, the bell might not be working.

Try the knocker. Almost reluctantly he did so. One part of him hoping the bell hadn't worked after he had finally made it; but most of him hoping it had and there just wasn't anybody in. There wasn't.

He forced himself to knock three times, but no one came to the door. After all that, he groaned, as he walked down the path, across the road and back towards the comfort and safety of his wall.

Never mind, his mind changed directions, now you've done it you can do it again. No way. I'm not going through that again. That was it. Nah, c'mon. Don't be stupid. Calm down. She wasn't in. Same thing applies. You want to know. You'll have to find out. Just try again later. He looked down at his watch. Tea'll be ready by now. I'll come back after.

He pulled himself off the wall again and turned for home. Perhaps it was a good thing she wasn't in. Gives me time to figure out somewhere to take her. Yeah. Good job that. He was continuing the process of convincing himself what a lucky break he'd just had when he reached the corner – and bumped straight into Trisha.

'You making a habit of this or something?' she demanded.

'Er . . . no . . . sorry.'

She just pulled a face that left him in no doubt what she thought of his mental state and walked past. Come on, he thought. This is it. Ask her. And to his own surprise he heard himself speaking.

'Er . . . you live round here?'

'No. On the moon. Why?'

'Oh . . . er . . . just wondered, like.'

'Now you know then, don't you?'

'Er . . . yeah . . . see you.' He had blown it. Her usual

110

belligerent attitude had fazed him. Still, can't blame her after the set-to's we've had.

As he walked away he threw a glance over his shoulder, but she was still walking away, not looking back. I'll do it tomorrow then. Don't fancy coming back tonight. Yeah. Tomorrow. Definitely tomorrow. Maybe.

As he turned the corner, Trisha looked back. She knew he lived miles away, and that he was probably there for a reason. She also knew that it was probably the same reason he'd been following her around the school for the past few weeks. She definitely knew she'd blown it. If she'd been able to appear a bit more friendly he might have finally asked her. But with their past record, who could blame her? Or him. She crossed the road, put her key in the door and looked back at the wall where she'd seen him waiting. She wished he'd get it over with.

Wonder if he'll come back later, she thought as she closed the door. Probably not. Maybe tomorrow. Maybe . . .

Z for Zachariah

ROBERT O'BRIEN

Put yourself in Ann Burden's position. She is sixteen, the lone survivor of a nuclear holocaust — or so she thinks. For over a year, since her family went in search of help soon after the bombing and did not return, Ann has not left the valley where she lives, a radiation-free island in the midst of nuclear wasteland.

Then one day a man comes into the valley, wearing a radiation-proof suit. Is he a friend and ally, as Ann first hopes, or the terrifying near-maniac she begins to suspect? Just as Adam was the first man on earth, so this man must be Zachariah, the last . . .

Told in diary form, Ann's account of the grim contest between them for survival makes a gripping and thought-provoking book, exploring the mental as well as the physical states necessary for survival in a nightmare future.

'This tale of humanity after atomic war brings to mind *Lord of the Flies* and will have a similar icy and compulsive effect on readers.' *Publishers' Weekly*